# Our Changing Lives

## A NOVEL

### by

### KENNETH SOLLITT

## SUNRISE BOOKS

1707 E Street
Eureka, California 95501
(707) 442-4004

Library of Congress Catalogue Card Number
86-60614

ISBN 0-940652-04-8

Dedicated to the Memory
of our first
great-grandson
Brett Daniel Nelson
September 11, 1983 · August 11, 1985

## ABOUT THE AUTHOR

As a boy growing up on a farm near Sibley, Iowa, (the Stebbinsville of **Ann of the Prairie**) Kenneth Sollitt was fascinated by stories the old timers told of daring homesteaders moving westward toward opportunity and freedom.

During his young manhood Kenneth spent many hours in the small Sibley Library poring over history books and pioneer novels. One of these, **A Lantern in Her Hand** by Bess Streeter Aldrich, made an impression on him that drew him to writing the stories he had heard as a youth. The first draft of **Ann of the Prairie** was written in longhand in the Sibley Library. His aunt's journals of her early days on the Iowa prairie helped give the emerging novel focus.

Dr. Sollitt graduated from Sibley High School, Sioux Falls (South Dakota) College, Colgate-Rochester Divinity School and has pastored churches in Vermont, Wisconsin, Illinois, Michigan and New Mexico. He was a script writer for the radio program "Victorious Living" and is a seven time winner of Freedom's Foundation Awards.

Dr. Sollitt and his wife, Maybelle, live in Rio Rancho, New Mexico.

## PUBLISHER'S PREFACE

The heartwarming story of the pioneering Bullard family began with **This Rough New Land,** volume one in the Ann of the Prairie series.

The sequel opens in the Spring of 1894 as the Bullards gather with their neighbors to celebrate the arrival of Ethan and Hilda Stone's new daughter Katrina.

From there events move on through those fragile years during which Ann grows from a girl to a young woman—encountering both the joy and heartbreak of romance, the discovery of books as lasting companions, continuing conflict with Pa, and the gentle realization that soon she must make decisions which will affect the rest of her life.

Above all, Ann learns that life is change and growth. And that God intended it so.

# PROLOGUE

The Spring of 1894 came to the Iowa prairie with a suddenness and sharpness that took my breath away. The warm Chinook wind melted the snow so fast that one day it was there and the next it wasn't. Almost overnight our pastures were carpeted in green with a generous sprinkling of yellow dandelions.

It was enough to fool a fifteen year old girl into leaving her shoes under the bed and going after the cows in the early morning barefooted. That was a mistake. I remember getting each cow up and standing where she had slept all night, to warm my feet a little before moving on.

I could see in anticipation the first purple crocuses appearing in the short pasture grass, then the buttercups, and in due time, the wild roses.

Meadowlarks swung on the cattails by the creek, singing their hearts out. The sweet smell of spring wafted on the warm morning breeze.

As I brought the cows up to the barn I was remembering another spring, four years ago when Papa, Mama, my four sisters and I moved into our unfinished house and started making a home out of it.

Mama had just brought little Mae into the world after the most terrible winter of her life, with no house to call home, living with neighbors and a husband who had moved her to this rough new Iowa land against her will.

Four years ago Papa was trying to get all the spring work done while it was still spring—plowing, planting, preparing a big vegetable garden, setting out trees for a windbreak, finishing the house, and a thousand other things. Papa worked hard and expected everyone else to work hard too. And that included Mama who was always doing things beyond her strength.

Papa was in the fields many hours each day, leaving the chores to us girls. And when he planted the windbreak he dug the holes and dropped the cuttings in, packing black earth around them, but we girls pumped and carried water all spring and summer to keep the little trees growing.

With no boys in the family we worked as hired men, except that we weren't men, and we worked without pay, often doing jobs that would wear heavily on the ablest man.

"Oh, but look at the place now!" I said as I opened the barnyard gate. It was a home—small, but a home. The barn was sturdy, the trees in the windbreak had grown tall and protective in just four years. The well gave us good water and a windmill was going up over it so we wouldn't have to pump water for the stock by hand.

The garden was productive, we had a young orchard bright with promise and cows, horses and chickens. We had a real home on the richest prairie soil in all the world!

During most of our early years we thought Papa had been wrong—we had all been certain this move to the rough Iowa prairie was a bad decision—but on such spring mornings nothing could have seemed more perfect than to be here at this, our house, on our land, tending our stock.

It was so easy to blame our troubles on Pa. At times he was so self centered, so tyrannical and often at the mercy of an unreasoning temper. I often thought I both loved him and hated him.

Pa was handsome. Tall, dark complected with slightly graying black hair and moustache, he seemed always to tower over the rest of us both emotionally and physically. But he never smoked, nor drank, nor played cards. He was religious in his own estimation but his boasting of being a self-made man left little doubt to whom he would give credit for his successes.

What a contrast was Mama! Much smaller and nicer to be around—in every way she was just what a Mama ought to be, quiet and obedient to her marriage vows, an ever-comforting presence. What she lacked in size she made up for in spiritual strength and courage. She had a round face, straight light brown hair which she wore swirled around and pinned on top of her head. She had soft blue eyes that could turn to steel if Papa mistreated one of us. We knew she would protect us from everything, including Papa.

We had heard the story of their marriage and how they moved from Virginia to Illinois in a covered wagon. Papa was a pioneer at heart. They had built up a good farm in Illinois. Elsie and I, Vina and Lucy were all born there. But no sooner was it a fine finished home than Papa bought a quarter section of Iowa soil and moved us out here—just to start all over again. To some it seemed like wasted years, to me it often seemed so. But anyone who said that could never have seen the Iowa prairie in spring—or at harvest time. At such times I could only thank God for Papa's pioneering spirit.

With the cows in the barn and fed their hay and grain, I slipped into the house, hoping no one would see my bare feet.

But Mama did.

"Landsakes, child, don't you know it's too early to go bare-footed. You'll catch your death of foolishness!" she said as she sat down to join the others for breakfast.

Papa answered for me, looking up briefly from his plate. "She's tough, Molly. She's a Bullard."

I sat down at my place at the kitchen table as Pa continued, "But shoes or no shoes, Ann, you and Vina have the milking to do, and you'd better not let a cow step on your bare feet. You aren't **that** tough!"

Between swallows of thickly buttered homemade bread, fried eggs and ham, Papa gave the orders for the day. "Since it's Saturday and no school, Ann when the milking is done, you ride the seeder today and be careful about overlapping. I want the forty acres we plowed and harrowed last fall planted by tonight. I'll fill the seeder the first time and get it ready for you, but you're big enough to handle those sacks of grain. Vina, you help your mother change the straw under the carpet. I'll be busy plowing the garden plot so Ma can start planting it. Lucy, you're too little to be worth much, but your time's coming. Molly, another slice of that ham, and fill my coffee cup."

It was enough to make me want to slow down eating my breakfast. The day and its work loomed ahead like a giant. But I knew to dawdle with my food would be even worse.

As I ate, I thought about Elsie my eldest sister's solution. She was eighteen and had to work harder than any of us. Finally, when she couldn't take it any longer she eloped with a neighbor boy, Jed Miller, and was expecting a baby in the fall.

I wouldn't let that happen to me. I had too many plans, even at age fifteen. I was a constant reader, wanting to learn new things, to travel, to become a writer. No, Elsie escaped through marriage, I would always escape through my daydreams...and my writing.

Vina was twelve that spring. She was the best looking of us girls—Papa's good looks, his black curly hair and dark eyes, but she had inherited Mama's disposition. She was almost always happy, smiling, loving—and mischievous.

Lucy was nine and certainly not as Papa had said, "too little to be worth much." She worked right along with the rest of us. She was a tomboy which occasionally got her into trouble. As did her temper, which she inherited from Papa.

Mae was barely more than a toddler with light curly hair and a sweetness that attracted all who saw her.

I sat at the table and thought of the day ahead and the years yet further ahead. We'd come so far in four years. But the future? What changes were ahead? What of our family, our school, church—our dear neighbors? I thought especially of Aunt Hilda, the feisty German lady we all loved so much. We would see her and Uncle Ethan tomorrow at the christening of their new baby. It would be a day of joy. And a day of rest.

God bless them...and us all, I prayed as I finished my last swallow of milk.

# CHAPTER I
## 1894

Aunt Hilda's baby was born in April, a beautiful little girl with blue eyes and taffy-colored fuzz on her round little head. She was the first baby christened in the new church. Katrina Marie Stone, named for Aunt Hilda's mother and Uncle Ethan's grandmother who had raised him after his mother died.

I had never been to a christening. It seemed very solemn for such a happy occasion, and all through the ceremony I thought about Elsie and her baby. Would Jed be disappointed if it wasn't a boy? One thing I was sure of. If it was a girl, Elsie would see to it that she never had to work like a boy as she had done.

After the christening everyone was invited to the Stone's house for refreshments before going home to prepare their own Sunday dinners. I didn't think they'd need much dinner after Aunt Hilda's "refreshments". The table was loaded with sandwiches, a big white cake with coconut icing, and two kinds of pie, with plenty of coffee. There was tea for the minister, served from a lovely china teapot she said her mother had brought from the Old Country.

"He must be English," Mrs. McCavity whispered to a group of ladies.

"I guess he could be," one of them said. "I hear he came from Philadelphia."

No one seemed in a hurry to go home. Aunt Hilda was so proud and happy she seemed to bounce instead of walk. If the new minister hadn't been there I'm sure she would have started a square-dance. She didn't agree with many in the community that dancing on Sunday was sinful, but I guess she wasn't sure how Rev. Pritchard felt about it and she didn't want to offend him.

I had thought a good deal lately about what was sinful and what wasn't. Sometimes sorting them out was difficult and puzzling. Several women and some of the men in our community considered dancing at any time "a tool of the devil."

7

They'd come to the gatherings but when the dancing started they'd find some excuse to leave, noses in the air, as if fleeing the devil himself. Neither Mama nor Papa felt that way about dancing. They taught us to respect the Sabbath and the House of God, and to do unto others as we would be done by.

On this special Sunday there was much eating and talking and laughter, but no dancing. The younger children were sent outside to play. I was old enough now to remain with the grown-ups and help Aunt Hilda with the serving. It was amusing to see the girls flock around Rev. Pritchard, each trying to get his attention. Some of the mothers were just as silly the way they behaved. They out-did each other praising their daughters, what good cooks they were and how well they sewed. I was sure Rev. Pritchard must have been more embarrassed than impressed. Uncle Ethan must have thought so too. He whispered to Papa, "I'd better rescue our preacher before those females smother him."

It was after three o'clock when Mama interrupted a discussion between Papa and Mr. Evans. "We should be starting home, Sam. All of us should. Hilda's had a long day. She must be worn out."

Papa agreed and sent me to gather up Vina, Lucy and Mae. When I came back Mama was talking with Rev. Pritchard. "We would like very much to have you and Mr. Evans come to our house for dinner next Sunday. I've spoken to Mr. Evans. He's agreeable if you are."

"It would be a pleasure, Mrs. Bullard." The eagerness in his voice made me think he'd just been waiting to be asked.

All the way home Papa was in high spirits. He teased Mama about getting to the preacher with her invitation before Mrs. Hughes did. "I'll lay you a bet the Reverend will be at *her* house the next Sunday. The way she was pushing Nellie onto the poor man was pretty silly."

"That's no way to talk, Sam. Nellie is a very nice girl."

"I didn't say she wasn't. But the preacher should have a right to make up his own mind. Doggonnit! The man just got here! Can't they give him time to catch his breath?"

Mama laughed. "Well, at least Mr. Evans might have a chance to catch his."

Until Rev. Pritchard came Mr. Evans had been the target.

Papa said not to worry about it, the man was more interested in cattle-breeding than in marriage. And it was Papa who advised him to concentrate on pure-bred cattle instead of farming. He thought farm work might be too strenuous for him until he got used to a more rugged way of life than a city schoolroom, and his health improved.

"It's sure to out here," he told Mr. Evans. "Give yourself a year or two in this good country air and you'll be a new man."

Mr. Evans had taken his advice. He hired a man who knew about cattle breeding to teach him what he needed to know, and to get things started until he had learned enough to handle them himself. He had new barns built with corrals and good wire fencing. He fixed up the house which was on the farm when he bought it. Now, Papa said, he had a fair-sized herd of pure-bred, and a good house. "Small, but all he needs. Pretty soon, with a good price for his stock, he can afford to tear it down and build a new one if he wants to."

It was at this time Mama had started supplying Mr. Evans with butter and eggs. He had one milk cow, she said, but she couldn't quite see him churning his own butter. And it seemed he had told her chickens were too much trouble. So, for more than a year now, Mama had been taking butter and eggs to him on her way to town each Saturday. If she didn't go to town she went to Mr. Evans' place anyway unless the weather was bad. Then he either did without or came for them himself.

One day, about a month or so before Rev. Prichard arrived, Mama took me with her. Mr. Evans invited us in. I was afraid Mama was going to say no, but she didn't. I wanted to see what his house was like. It *was* very nice, and not nearly as small as Papa had said. There was a roomy kitchen which also served as his dining-room, a big sitting-room with a huge fireplace, and a bedroom I suppose; I didn't see it but there was a door that probably led into it. What impressed me was his books. I expected he would have a lot, but not *so many!*

"Please excuse the clutter, Mrs. Bullard," he said when he showed us into the sitting-room. "I've been unpacking books. It's beginning to look like they or I will have to move out."

"I can't imagine books cluttering any room," Mama said, then exclaimed, "Why, you've performed a miracle with this old house, Mr. Evans. You truly have!"

"It's comfortable enough, but I'm going to have to build onto it very soon, I'm afraid. You see, the books that have arrived are only part of my collection. There are several more boxes which will come with the furniture when it is shipped. I'm going to need a library, and a rather large one at that."

We sat on the sofa and looked about while he went to the kitchen for coffee. Books were everywhere. One whole wall of shelves filled with them, and they were stacked on tables and chairs. One box was still to be unpacked.

Mr. Evans came back with a tray. There was milk for me, and three pieces of coconut cake. "It's quite good, really," he assured us. "I tested it first. One of my neighbors was kind enough to donate it to my bachelor existence."

The conversation returned to his books. "I very much need your advice, Mrs. Bullard, about the library. I must get it built before any more books arrive, but I'm not sure which side of the house would be best for it."

Mama got up and went to the windows on opposite sides of the room. "May I make a suggestion?"

"Please do. I'd be very grateful."

"Why not make this room your library? If you take full advantage of the wall space there will be plenty of room for more bookcases, and with the big fireplace, this should make a perfectly delightful library."

"Yes. Yes. I see now how easily that could be done. With less furniture in here there would be ample room for bookcases."

"And when you are ready to add to the house, you could build onto the east side which would give you a fine view even without landscaping. There would be plenty of room for a garden if you want one and have time for it." She came back to the sofa and sat down. "But those are only my suggestions, remember. I'm not exactly experienced in fixing up bachelor houses!"

Mr. Evans laughed. "I should say you do very well in the matter, Mrs. Bullard." Then he sobered. "Perhaps I give too much importance to a library. After all this *is* a stock-breeding farm."

"No, I don't think so. I'm sure you've always spent a good deal of time in your library. Reading is important to you."

"Sometimes too much, I'm afraid. At least that was the doctor's opinion in New York."

"Out here, it's true, one doesn't have much time for books. The land makes constant demands. But I think a library is as necessary to you as a parlor is to a woman. Mr. Bullard was quite convinced we didn't need a parlor but now that we have it he spends more time in it than the girls do." She smiled. "There must be a moral somewhere in all this but I haven't had time to figure it out."

"Perhaps Ann can tell us what it is," he teased, turning to me. "We haven't given her a chance to say a word."

I was still too awed by him and his many books to tell him what I really thought. How could I tell him I'd never known anyone who had so many books he needed a special room for them? Mama came to my rescue.

"Ann would much prefer a library to a parlor, I'm afraid. She's the bookworm of the family. If she had her way she'd be reading all the time."

He seemed pleased about that. He asked me what I had read, what I liked best. I mentioned some of the books, and said how much I enjoyed the reading at Literary Society, and his recitations. Then Mama said it was time we got on our way, she had a lot to do in town. He thanked her again for her suggestions about his house and the library, then took my hand. "I'm *very* glad you're a bookworm, Miss Ann. That should make us friends, wouldn't you say? And friends share their books. Would you like to take one today?"

I looked at Mama and she replied, "It's all right, dear."

I went to the bookcase with him and tried to see all the titles and beautiful bindings at once. "There are so many . . ."

He took one from the shelf. It was bound in green leather with the title in gold letters. *Vanity Fair*, by William Makepeace Thackeray. "I think you will enjoy this."

Mama glanced at it. "Isn't that a little advanced for her?"

"I don't think so. Ann seems to have read a good deal more than most girls her age. Besides, books *should* stretch the mind."

I thanked him. "I'll take very good care of it, Mr. Evans."

"It's value is in the writing, not the binding. When you've finished it you must come again and tell me how you like it."

11

He went with us to the surrey. I wrapped the book in my scarf and could scarcely wait to get home to start reading it. For the next two weeks I hurried through my studies at night so I could read a chapter before Mama sent us to bed.


I was thinking about the book, which I still hadn't finished, as we drove home from the christening. And about Mr. Evans. Now that Rev. Pritchard would be sharing his house would he ever have time to talk about books with me? Or even remember he had invited me to come back to see him? I didn't care whether Rev. Pritchard came to our house next Sunday for dinner, or went to Mrs. Hughes'. But I was glad Mr. Evans was coming. Maybe I'd get a chance to discuss *Vanity Fair* with him. I had only a few more chapters to read. If I hurried through my chores tonight, I might be able to finish the book. On Sundays I didn't have to study.

Mama baked a chocolate cake the following Sunday morning before we left for church. The chicken was cut up ready for frying, vegetables peeled and put in crocks of cold water ready for cooking while the chicken fried. A "leaf" had been added to the table in the dining room. It was already set with her best linen tablecloth, china and silverware when we came downstairs for breakfast. She must have been up since dawn. Papa did the morning chores by himself so we could help Mama straighten up the house and dust the parlor furniture. She wanted everything spick and span for our guests.

The church was again crowded. There was no doubt now that Rev. Pritchard was well liked, both for his sermons and himself. Papa said he saw several families there that hadn't been near the schoolhouse meetings for months.

When we got home from church Papa took Rev. Pritchard and Mr. Evans into the parlor while we finished preparing dinner. Mama was very proud to have the parlor, even if it was "temporary," and a proper dining-room. I wondered if Mr. Evans remembered what she had said about the importance of a parlor. He hadn't been in our parlor before.

During dinner Rev. Pritchard discussed plans for Easter Services, two weeks away. "We haven't too much time to prepare for them. I was wondering if you might spare some time,·

Mrs. Bullard, to assist me in selecting members for a choir. You're probably familiar with the singing talents in the community."

"I'd be glad to. Several of the women, and men too, have excellent voices. Let's see. There's Mrs. Rogers and . . ."

"Forgive me for interrupting. I've been thinking it might be best to select choir members from the young people of the parish, give them a more active part in our church work." He smiled across the table at me. "Perhaps Miss Ann, for one, and Miss Hughes."

"Ann's still a little young for that responsibility, Rev. Pritchard. However I think a young-people's choir would be desirable. I'm sure we can find enough good voices among the older girls."

Papa agreed. "You're less likely to step on toes, too. Can't you just imagine what would happen, Molly, if Mrs. McCavity *weren't* selected?"

Rev. Pritchard smiled. Mama said nothing. Nor did Mr. Evans.

"Do you think it would be possible to get these young women together for practice this week?" Rev. Pritchard asked.

"It might be. Do I understand you want only female voices?"

"For the choir, yes. I thought we might use the male voices for a glee club." He glanced around the table. "I'd like to know what all of you think about that. I planned to use the choir for morning service, and the glee club for evening service and special events."

Papa quickly agreed with the idea. He had a good singing voice and liked to use it. Mr. Evans said it seemed like a fine idea. Mama said, "It would certainly be an inducement to get folks in for evening service. Some of them do have to come quite a distance."

That seemed to settle the matter of choir and glee club. Papa now mentioned the parsonage. "I was talking with Ben Miller before church this morning. He and the rest of the Board agree the parsonage should be started as soon as possible. Get it finished before all of us are too busy with harvest."

"Rev. Pritchard will doubtless approve of that," Mr. Evans said, smiling. "Although please understand *I'm* not going to be happy about losing him. He's very handy with the frying pan and dish pan."

"Don't you believe him," Rev. Pritchard insisted. "After a week of burned bacon, Jim, I notice you were pretty glad to take over the cooking yourself. But I'll admit I'm rather good at dish-washing. My mother saw to that when I was a boy."

There was much laughter and teasing back and forth. I'd never heard anyone call Mr. Evans by his first name before. Even Mama and Papa always referred to him by his full name and they'd known him a lot longer than Rev. Pritchard had. But I supposed two men couldn't live in the same house and not use first names. Even if one was a college professor and the other a minister.

After dinner Mama served coffee in the parlor. It was the first time she had used her beautiful silver coffee pot with matching creamer and sugar bowl since we left Saunemin. They were her most treasured possessions, a wedding present from Grandma and Grandpa. She had had little chance to use them living on farms and moving every time Papa got the idea to pioneer.

The talk now was about where the parsonage would stand. The Board had made a down payment on the lot next to the church at the time it was built. The rest of it would be paid off by donations and social events.

"If everyone helps with the building," Papa said, "the parsonage could be ready by June."

That was fine, I thought, but who would help Mr. Evans build his library?

Mama was up early Monday morning. She had her washing on the line by the time we finished our chores and were ready for school.

"I wish you'd hitch the team to the surrey, Sam, before you leave for the fields," she said at breakfast. "I'll take the girls to school and then round up those choir members for Rev. Pritchard."

Papa no longer objected to Mama using the surrey. Sometimes he was so agreeable about almost everything he seemed like a different person. He didn't lose his temper so often and usually accepted whatever Mama suggested without complaining. The biggest surprise was that he said nothing about returning to the hardware store once the crops were in. He seemed quite satisfied to let Donald Matthews and Mama

14

handle the business. And it was prospering. I couldn't help hearing their discussions about it, usually after we had gone upstairs leaving them in the kitchen. Papa liked a "snack" before going to bed.

Mama seemed happier now than she had been in a long time. For us girls it was the best time we had known since moving to Iowa. We no longer were expected to work in the fields. We helped with chores but when there was heavy work to be done, more than Papa could do alone, he hired someone to do it. At last we were beginning to live the way Mama had always wanted us to live.

The new choir met for practice on Wesdnesday. How Mama had been able to include every unmarried young woman who could carry a tune was a kind of miracle, I thought. Since she, not Rev. Pritchard, had made the selections the older women who had good voices were not offended. If they were, it was Mama's fault, not our new minister, and the community was not large enough to offer too many candidates. Preparations for Easter services went forward with much enthusiasm.

Saturday morning, when Vina and I came in from doing the chores, Mama said, "Eat your breakfast, girls, then change your clothes. I'm taking you to town with me today to get your Easter hats."

"Aren't we going to go to Mr. Evans' with butter and eggs?" Eager as I was for a new hat, I still didn't want to miss the visit to Mr. Evans even if it wasn't the same now the minister was there too.

"We can do that on our way."

Vina was so excited she scracely touched her breakfast. Lucy asked, "What about me, Mama?"

"You'll have to stay here with Mae, dear. But I'll bring you both a new hair ribbon for Easter,"

"Hair ribbons are for *kids*," she complained. "I want a hat too. I'm big enough."

Mama looked at her for a minute. Lucy *was* almost as tall as Vina. And a lot rounder!

"Yes, I believe you are dear. We'll all go and take Mae with us. She can have the new hair ribbon."

"Won't Papa be mad if we all go? Who will make lunch for him?" Vina asked.

"He can manage alone for one day. Hurry along, now, all of you."

We went first to Mr. Evans place and left the basket. He met us in the back yard so we didn't even get out. I guess he knew we were in a hurry. Maybe he also knew it was a special occasion. In town, Mama tied the team to the hitching rail in front of the store. "You girls will have to wait while I go over business matters with Donald .Then we'll see about your hats."

"May we see the store, too, Mama?" Lucy asked.

"I guess it would be better for you to wait inside. Come along! But I don't want you disturbing us."

We promised. All of us were curious to see what Donald Matthews looked like. The way Mama talked about him, how smart he was and how well he took care of the store, he must be a lot nicer than some of the other young men in town.

As we entered, he left a stack of papers he was working on and came to greet us. "Good morning, Mrs. Bullard. You're earlier than usual." He shook hands with her.

"Yes. We have some special shopping to do today. Easter bonnets for my girls". She introduced each of us by name.

Mr. Matthews bowed and smiled. "A real pleasure to meet you."

We sat on a bench near the front of the store while Mama went over accounts with him. Vina became impatient. She kept changing her seat, bouncing from the bench to a chair and back again. Mama paid no attention to her but Mr. Matthews did. Several times he looked up and smiled. I couldn't tell whether he was annoyed or interested. Vina acted like she wanted to be noticed, and he *was* nice looking. He was taller than Mama and rather thin, but his wavy straw-colored hair was so thick it made him seem even taller. He didn't look any older than Jed, but his general manner was brisk and business-like. But I thought his eyes did light up a little when he smiled at Vina. She *was* pretty.

When the business was finished Mr. Matthews walked to the door with us. "I hope you will bring your charming daughters with you again soon, Mrs. Bullard." To us he said, "And I'm sure your bonnets will be the prettiest ones in church on Easter Sunday."

16

On the way to Miss Millie's Hat Shop Vina remarked, "He's nice, Mama."

So! She *had* been trying to get him to notice her. Maybe Gus Gruder was going to have a rival.

We finally selected our hats after "trying on" for almost an hour. Mama waited patiently, approving our final selections. "You'll all make Papa and me very proud on Easter Sunday."

"Why can't Easter be tomorrow, Mama?" Vina asked. "I just *can't* wait a whole week to wear my hat."

"No one can change the time of Easter, honey." She explained that Easter was always on the first Sunday following the first full moon after March 21st. "So you'll have to wait, I'm afraid."

"I guess so, but it's going to be awful hard."

"And while you're waiting, young lady, you might try to remember Easter stands for something more important than showing off a new hat."

We counted the days and tried on our new hats a dozen times. And prayed it wouldn't rain on Easter Sunday. It didn't. The day was bright and clear and quite warm for that time of year. When we arrived at the church, dressed in our new clothes, the hitching rail already was lined with buggies, surreys and springwagons. Rev. Pritchard would preach to a full church today.

We followed Mama and Papa down the aisle to our seats next to Uncle Ethan and Aunt Hilda and their children. Everyone seemed to be watching us. Maybe our hats *were* the prettiest in the church. As soon as we were seated I looked around. Everyone else was dressed up too. And the church decorations were beautiful. Mrs. Phillips was at the organ on the rostrum. The choir girls were seated at the right of the pulpit, dressed in white with flowered hats. Rev. Pritchard stood behind the pulpit waiting for late arrivals to be seated. Gradually the house became quiet. He lifted his arms. The choir and congregation stood. Mrs. Philips struck a chord on the organ. The song seemed to fill the room as the congregation joined with the choir.

"Christ the Lord is risen . . . . ."

# CHAPTER II
## 1894

April departed with heavy rains. May danced in on gentle winds. The land blossomed under Nature's magic touch. Bright yellow dandelions, clumps of black-eyed-susans, and gold and purple crocus dotted the meadows. Orchards and plum thickets were bursting with pink and white blossoms. Lilacs filled the air with their delicate fragrance.

This extravagant beauty each morning was almost more than I could bear. Sometimes too much beauty was like a pain in the heart. The leaves of the big cottonwood glistened in the sunlight, whispering to themselves. Were these secrets of the night, or promises for a new day? The windbreak stood tall like a green wall. Far beyond growing grain rippled in silvery-green waves.

Driving the cows to pasture on mornings such as these was a joy. It was good to be alive. Good to feel the wind in my hair, the sun's fingers touch my face. The cows walked slowly stopping to munch on tender, new grass. I had time to think about many things. I thought how much our lives had changed, and tried to remember the exact time and cause of the change but I couldn't. The new pattern of our lives seemed to emerge from those first hard years we had spent here, like a flower growing out of the dark soil. But whatever the reason or cause, I knew Mama had had more to do with it than Papa. Her gentle patience and determination had done more than Papa's storming about trying to force things to his way. Now, he, too, was learning that his way was not always the best.

Some mornings, on the way to the pasture, I counted the exciting things that were happening in our community. The parsonage foundation was laid and the walls were going up. Mr. Evans had started to build on the new rooms he had talked about with Mama. I wondered if he would make his sitting-room into a library, as she had suggested. Since Rev. Pritchard had moved into his house, Mama had taken me with her only once when she delivered butter and eggs. That was just before Easter, and Mr. Evans had been too busy to talk about the books he was going to lend me. But school would soon be out and I'd have more time to read. Perhaps I could ask Mama to remind Mr. Evans about the books.

The days passed. I decided it wouldn't be proper for Mama to ask about books for me. She, too, was very busy these days. Soon I found other interests. A warm June sun ripened the grain and brought more flowers. School ended for the summer. Rev. Pritchard moved into the new parsonage. Old Mrs. Wiley who had no kinfolk, came out from town to be his housekeeper. She kept his house neat, cooked his meals, and kept a watchful eye on the unmarried girls who fluttered around him hopeful of special attention. I thought she need not have worried too much. Rev. Pritchard seemed quite able to take care of himself in such matters. He accepted Sunday dinner invitations from their parents but he gave no more attention to one young woman than to another.

Papa often laughed about all this. "For a preacher, he sure knows how to handle women. The more he pushes them away, the better they like him. One of these days he'll make his choice."

"He's not trying to make them like him except as a minister, Sam," Mama said. "I've a good mind to speak to some of the mothers about the way their daughters behave. You don't see our girls acting so silly."

"They're young yet. Give 'em time, Molly. Give 'em time!"

Mama didn't answer him. She might have had I not been in the room. But I could have told her I'd never act that way, and Vina was too interested in Gus and maybe Donald Matthews.

The addition to Mr. Evans' house was finished about the middle of June. Mama surprised me on Saturday when she said she was taking me with her to deliver the weekly produce. "We are both invited to see his new rooms and have tea with him."

"Did he really invite me, Mama?"

"He certainly did. 'Bring Miss Ann, please'. Those were his exact words."

Usually the delivery was made in the morning, but today it would be afternoon at a proper time for tea. I spent an hour fixing my hair and trying on dresses before I decided my yellow chambray would be proper for the occasion. Mama said it was. I noticed she was wearing one of her best dresses, too. "It's not every day a woman and her daughter have tea with a college professor," she said, laughing. We took the surrey, and all the way to Mr. Evans' farm Mama was in a gay mood. And I understood how much she missed the way of life she had had in Virginia.

Mr. Evans was waiting at the gate to greet us when we drove in. He waved a hand toward the addition as we walked toward the house. "It's getting to be a regular manor house, wouldn't you say?" Mama emphatically agreed.

He had followed her suggestion. The addition was on the east side, and it looked much too big for one room. At the back stoop he asked us to wait a moment. He took the basket of butter and eggs inside and came back. "Today we enter by the front door," he said proudly. I'd never seen him in such a gay mood.

There was a wide front porch across the added structure. From it you could see great stretches of open fields, now golden with ripening grain. Far off the land dipped toward the road, then rose again seeming to reach to the horizon. Close by were the beginnings of a garden already marked with a picket fence and rock-bordered path.

"As you see, I took your advice, Mrs. Bullard. The view is, indeed, superb. But come inside. See what I've done with the rest of the house. I'm most eager for your opinion."

We stepped through the doorway into another world.

The new sitting-room was quite large and much more elegant than Mama's or Grandma's parlors. The furniture must be what he had had shipped from New York. I'd never seen anything so grand. The rug was thick and silky-soft, with designs of many colors, not flowers like most rugs.

Mama exclaimed, "An Oriental rug in an Iowa farm house! Mr. Evans, you'll be the envy of every woman in the community. It's very beautiful."

He smiled and thanked her. "I suppose it is a trifle out of place here, however. But I couldn't bring myself to part with it. It was a gift from a Turkish student I had taught to speak English."

Just *knowing* someone from a far-away place like Turkey

was awesome. I was completely convinced now that Mr. Evans must know everything.

"Come. Let me show you the new library. I'm enormously proud of it."

At first I saw only the books. There must be hundreds of them! They filled three big bookcases, floor to ceiling, one on each side of the fireplace and another on a side wall. In the corner created by the joining bookcases was a beautifully carved table on which stood a lamp with a colored glass shade. Beside the table was a high-backed green-leather chair. (How could you make leather green?) Opposite these, on the other side of the fireplace, were two big chairs covered with dark red brocade like the scarf on Grandma's center table. In front of the fireplace was a long low table of dark wood bordered with gold. Across the room was a divan covered with soft yellow brocade. The carpet was much like the one in the sitting-room but with a different design.

Mama stood as if spellbound. "My goodness! How could anyone *not* approve of all this, Mr. Evans? Why, you've actually brought English manor-house charm to the Iowa prairies. You've every right to be proud."

He thanked her. "I *am* pleased with it. And I'm not forgetting that much of its charm is due to your suggestions, for which I'm most grateful. And now if you'll excuse me a moment I'll see to our tea. A butler is not one of my luxuries here. Perhaps, in time . . . ."

Mama laughed, "I wouldn't be a bit surprised!"

We sat in the big chairs and sipped tea, and ate the raisin cookies Mama had brought as a special surprise. "I know the tradition is a loaf of bread as a housewarming gift, but I thought you'd prefer cookies."

"Correct, as always."

They talked a while of community affairs before he remarked, "Now I should like to show Ann some of my special books."

I walked beside him as we explored the many shelves. How beautiful the bindings were! And there were so many books I couldn't begin to remember all the titles. No wonder he needed this special room for them. Mama relaxed, watching and seeming as impressed as I was.

21

"It must have taken you many years to collect these," she said. "Did you have them bound? They appear to be the work of a very fine craftsman."

"Yes. Most of these were done in England, but I finally found several European artisans in New York. Fewer and fewer people, I'm afraid, are using their fine talents. We are in too great hurry so much of the time in this country."

Too soon, it was time to go. He had selected two books for me. "These are not so serious, my dear. Summer is a time for enjoyment."

I looked at the titles. *The Legend of Sleepy Hollow* and *The Adventures of Tom Sawyer*. I thought they sounded more suitable for boys.

"These are American classics, Ann. They should be a part of everyone's reading program. I'm sure you will enjoy them."

He went to the surrey with us and thanked us for coming. "I hope you will come often." He smiled at me. "We've a lot of reading to do, young lady."


At Literary Society the following Friday, most of the evening was given to plans for a Fourth of July celebration. There would be patriotic songs and recitations, and a special play, followed by fireworks and refreshments. After these, square-dancing. It would be the biggest celebration the community had had.

After the meeting I was waiting outside for Mama and Papa to finish a discussion about decorations. It was cooler here. The weather had turned very warm this past week. Papa said it was unseasonable, but too early to worry about cyclones. We could use some rain though, he said. I hoped it would wait a while.

I was thinking about this when Tom Simpson came out. "It sure is hot in there." He looked up at the clear sky. The stars were coming out like a thousand little lamps. "It's nice here though, don't you think?"

I agreed it was a beautiful summer night. "I hope it stays this nice for the Fourth. It would be awful if it rained, wouldn't it?"

"It sure would. Imagine trying to shoot fireworks in a rain

storm." We laughed about that. "I bet no one ever did that," Tom said. "Anyway, if it does rain we can still have the dance and the rest of the program."

"Well, I'm going to pray it doesn't. I want to wear my new dress."

"Then I'll pray, too. I want to see your new dress." And we laughed again.

Pretty soon he said slowly, "Are you going to the dance with anyone, Ann?"

"Sure. With Mama and Papa and Vina." I knew what he meant but I wanted him to say it.

"Could I . . . I mean would you . . . let me take you? I mean call for you in my own buggy?"

My heart was pounding. Papa would never let me go with him alone. Not unless Mama said it was all right. But if I told Tom that he might think I didn't want to go with him. I couldn't risk that.

"I'll be pleased to go to the dance with you, Tom. And if Mama says it is all right for you to call for me in your own buggy, I'd like that, too."

"Shall I ask her?"

I wasn't sure which was proper, but if Mama was going to forbid me to go alone with Tom I'd prefer she said so to me, not to him. "Maybe I'd better ask her. Then she'll know I want to go."

There wasn't time to say more. Mama and Aunt Hilda came out, and soon we were on the way home. The stars suddenly seemed bigger and brighter. I didn't have a chance to talk to Mama about Tom's invitation until the next morning. She took a while to answer.

"Tom's a very nice boy. I see no reason why he shouldn't take you to the dance if you want to go with him. But I'll have to talk to Papa about it."

"Do you *have* to, Mama? You know how strict he is and I do so much want to go with Tom."

"Yes, dear, I have to. I think maybe Papa also realizes you are growing up."

Whatever she said to Papa must have convinced him. He gave his consent. When I saw Tom at church on Sunday I told him it was all right for him to call for me. And the following

Saturday when Mama went to town I went along to get the new dress she had promised me. It would be my first grown-up dress, and Mama let me select the material, and the pattern. It was pink voile with lacey ruffles about the yoke and at the bottom of the skirt, and it was longer than my other dresses. I felt really grown up in it and could scarcely wait for the Fourth.

All the next week Vina and Lucy teased me. "Ann has a feller! Ann has a feller!" they'd sing over and over and giggle.

"That will be enough of that, young ladies!" Mama scolded. "It won't seem so funny when the shoe is on your foot."

We had an early supper the night of the big party. Mama helped me with my beautiful new dress. "There now. Stand back and let me look at you. My, you do look pretty, dear. Like strawberries and cream. Tom is going to be mighty proud to take *you* to the dance."

She left me alone to make sure Papa and the others were ready, and to receive Tom when he knocked. He would wait, properly, in the parlor talking to Mama and Papa for a while. After a few impatient minutes I went downstairs, walking slowly with grown-up dignity. Tom stood up as I came into the parlor and looked at me like he'd never seen me before. "Gee!" he said, then quickly recovered his own dignity. "Good evening, Ann."

We sat a few minutes, both of us uncomfortable. Papa kept looking at me but he didn't say anything about my new dress. Finally he took out his watch and glanced at it. "I guess we'd better get started, Molly," he said, getting up. "Are the other girls ready?"

As soon as we were in Tom's buggy alone he said, "You sure do look pretty, Ann. You sure do!" He slapped the reins sharply. "Getty-up there, Ruby! I'm taking the prettiest girl in the county to the dance."


As summer deepened so did our lives. We were not rich in the way Vina was sure we would be when Mama bought the buildings and opened up the hardware store again. But we had more of the good things that made life pleasant and happy. One morning in late July Papa drove over to the Rogers'

24

farm. When he came back he had two new horses tied to the back of the springwagon. One was a sorrel mare with a white face, the other black as night. Mama and Vina and I were sitting under the cottonwood tree cutting up string beans and beets for canning, when he drove in at the back gate.

"What magnificent animals, Sam!" Mama exclaimed. "Where did you get them?"

"Hank Rogers made me such a good price I couldn't afford to turn it down. It's time the girls learned to ride anyway. Hank says these mares are gentle enough for a child to ride."

"Well, we'll have to see about that. They look pretty spirited to me." She put down her crock of beets and went to examine them.

Vina and I looked at each other. The very idea of having our *own* horses was too good to believe. Papa sure had changed! We ran to the wagon before Mama could talk him out of letting us have them.

"If Mr. Rogers says they're gentle, Mama, they must be," I urged.

"Are they really for us, Papa?" Vina asked.

"Only if you agree to take care of 'em."

"Oh, we will! We will!"

"And you're not to ride unless Mama or I says you can. Is that understood?"

"Yes, Papa. We promise, don't we, Ann?" I repeated the promise.

"All right. Ann is the oldest so she has first choice."

I did not need to consider. The black mare was the most beautiful animal I'd ever seen. Besides, she looked like she had more spunk, and I liked that.

"Goody! Goody!" Vina cried, dancing up and down. "I wanted the sorrel anyway."

Mama laughed. "So everybody's happy. But mind what Papa said. There is to be *no* riding without permission. And *no* permission until you've learned to ride properly."

I went to the black mare and ran my hands over her sleek sides. She turned at my touch and nudged me gently with her nose. "See! She likes me, Papa. She knows she belongs to me. I'm going to call her Midnight."

He laughed. "Not very original."

Vina's name for the sorrel was no more original than mine, but it was suitable: *Golden*. Her coat *did* seem to glow in the sunlight.

For a while even the books Mr. Evans lent me were forgotten. Papa gave us our first riding lessons, then turned us over to Cyrus Crump, our hired man. Soon we were able to take the horses out by ourselves, but only for short rides at first. We fed and watered and curried them faithfully. Too faithfully, Papa finally said. "They're getting fat and lazy. And you're wearing holes in their hides with that curry-comb."

At last the time came when we were allowed to ride beyond sight of the house. Even Papa admitted we were "good horse-women". Mama still warned us to be careful. She was spending more time now at Elsie's place so we didn't have too much time for riding anywhere. I did some of the cooking, and most of the housework was left to Vina and me. Mama could no longer take the time to deliver butter and eggs to Mr. Evans. Finally she agreed to let me take them. It occurred to me Mr. Evans would have come for them himself if he had known how busy Mama was, but I didn't mention this. It was an errand I looked forward to all week.

Midnight soon knew the way. She'd amble along slowly so as not to break the eggs. Mr. Evans seemed to know her hoofbeats after a while. He would come out the moment we rode into the yard and take the basket and help me down. Then he'd bring water and oats for Midnight and tie her up under a shade-tree before we went into the house. Always there was ice-tea, with cream and sugar, or lemonade. Sometimes there was cake or cookies supplied by one of his neighbors. We would talk for a while about the book I had been reading, and if I had finished it he would select another to take back with me. Sometimes he would let me make my own selection, but if he didn't approve he would explain why and suggest another.

"Have you really read *all* these books, Mr. Evans?" I asked one day when he hesitated to approve the book I had selected.

"Yes, most of them, that is. Some I have read several times. They're like old friends." He went to the bookcase on the side wall. "This whole shelf, however, contains books waiting

26

to be read. I like to think of them as new friends whom I hope to know very well in time."

I looked at the two tall bookcases which held the books he had read, and thought of the years it must have taken him. How long would it take him to read the rest of them? How long would it take me to read the books on even one shelf of one bookcase? Suddenly it didn't matter how long it might take.

He picked up another book he thought more suitable for me now. "This is one of my oldest friends. I find a singular joy in sharing a book-friend I cherish with you, Ann. Too few girls your age have the capacity to appreciate good literature. You have that, my dear, to an extraordinary degree. Don't ever lose it. It will bring you riches beyond price, riches of the mind and heart to treasure forever." He broke off. "Forgive me for behaving like a professor!"

I thanked him for wanting to share his books with me. "Do you think I'll *ever* be able to read even half of them?"

"Many of them would not interest you. Nor would they be suitable reading for you unless you decide to become a teacher some day. Textbooks and manuals, you know. Not very exciting reading for a pretty girl. Soon you'll have other interests beside reading, my dear. Marriage and a family with a home of your own. So we shall see that you do all the reading you can before that happens. Do you agree?" I nodded. I could think of nothing to say.

All the way home I thought about what he had said. Elsie and Jed seemed very happy together, and both were excited about having a baby of their own. Would I feel that way some day? I didn't think I would, not if it meant never having time to read. Elsie had worked hard before she got married, and now she worked just as hard with no time to do the things she had dreamed about. I liked Tom Simpson and went to dances with him when he asked me. He had nice manners and I knew he liked me. But if I got married I'd probably never get to see big cities and libraries and museums and all the places I'd dreamed about. Still, I thought, it might be very nice to be married to a man like Mr. Evans. We'd live in his big beautiful house and I'd read all his books and we could talk about them whenever we wanted to. I'd have no farm chores to do. I'd wear beautiful clothes like the ladies in the books I had read, and serve tea in the library when our friends came to call. Or we'd go riding together across the meadows on spirited horses, the way lovers did in English novels. And Mr. Evans *was* English. Oh yes! *that* would be the grandest kind of life!

I stopped Midnight and sat very still. Were these just foolish dreams? No. no, they had to be more than that! Maybe I was in love. I'd never felt like this before, so happy and alive all over. Even the sky was suddenly bluer, the grass greener.

"It's true!" I cried to the open prairies, "I'm in love! I'm in love!" I sang the words to the rhythm of Midnight's hoof-beats. The wind caught my song and carried it in endless echo.

I floated through the summer days on snow-white clouds of pure happiness. Some part of me did my chores, made beds, washed dishes, curried and watered and fed Midnight, ate and slept. But the best part of me was on a far-away cloud, high above ordinary things, waiting only for Saturday. Seeing Mr. Evans at church on Sundays was not the same. There he belonged to everyone. But on Saturdays he belonged to me!

My love for him was my secret held close to my heart. I couldn't talk to anyone about it, not Vina or even Elsie or Mama. To keep it secret I could not refuse to go to parties and dances with Tom. Mama and Papa approved of him. I didn't think they would approve of the way I felt about Mr. Evans. They would think him too old for me, or that I was silly thinking he loved me as I loved him. But I *knew* he cared. Sometimes in a square dance I'd have him for a partner and my heart would pound so hard I was sure he could hear it. When the dance ended he would bow and tell me how beautifully I danced. For the rest of the evening I pretended I was dancing with him, no matter that it was Tom, or Will, or Zeke.

The hot August days drifted by. Life went on around me— life I was a part of, yet wasn't. Haying, threshing and corn husking, vegetable and fruit canning, even the bloody business of butchering which I hated. I could endure all these because my heart was with him, and once each week I could spend an hour with him in his beautiful house and talk of things we both loved.

September came with cooler winds and rain to drench the parched fields. But on sunny days soft breezes played tag in the high branches of our windbreak. Marigolds and zinnias and hollyhocks filled Mama's flower beds with bright colors. Nights there was a chill in the air.

On a Sunday in early October the talk after church was about the new teacher. Mrs. Phillips, who had continued to teach after her marriage to Elmer Phillips, had notified the Board when school was out in June that she would not be able to teach in the fall. Everyone knew she was going to have a baby. All summer the Board had searched and argued over the qualifications of several applicants. Now they had hired one, a young woman from St. Louis. The community buzzed with speculation and curiosity. Would she be pretty? the unmarried girls asked among themselves. They wanted no more competition with the only two eligible men in the community. The older women were concerned for different reasons.

"Well, I just hope she won't be uppity, comin' from St. Louis with all its fancy ways," Mrs. Seton remarked loud enough for everyone to hear. "She'll soon find farm life's no picnic. We're simple, hard-working folks. We ain't got time for fancy parties and the like."

I smiled. Mrs. Seton believed anything that wasn't plain or difficult was sinful—like dancing and parties and pretty clothes.

"I'm sure Miss Engles knows we are farmers," Mama said. "She didn't have to come here unless she wanted to."

"Don't be so sure about that, Molly," Mrs. Seton went on in a high-pitched voice. "*Some* of them city teachers ain't all they're supposed to be!" She glanced slyly at Mama. "Could be she *had* to leave St. Louis."

"Ellie Seton, I'm surprised at you!" Mama replied severely. "You haven't even seen the woman and already you've marked her 'bad'. Stop imagining things! The Board decided she is a proper teacher for us. I'm sure she is."

A few others in the community shared Mrs. Seton's fears. Anyone from St. Louis just *couldn't* be a good woman! Not if she was single and willing to go traipsing off somewhere the first time she was asked. But most accepted the Board's good judgment and prepared to welcome Miss Engles. School was to open the middle of October. Miss Engles would arrive a few days before. Arrangements had been made for her to board and room with the Hughes family.

Silas Hughes, being Chairman of the Board, received a telegram from Miss Engles the following Tuesday saying she would arrive on Thursday. He stopped by our house that afternoon to show the telegram to Mama.

"By rights Mrs. Hughes and I should meet the train. But I'm in the middle of butchering and I can't leave. And you know Mrs. Hughes is scared to death to drive anywhere by herself. Could you go with her, take your surrey? He smiled. "It *is* the nicest in the community and we want to make a good impression on the new teacher, don't we?"

Mama laughed. "After that piece of blarney, how can I refuse? Better let me take this telegram. Mrs. Hughes doesn't need to go unless she wants to."

"That's mighty nice of you, Molly. She *did* want to stay home and see everything's ready for her."

I begged Mama to take me along on Thursday morning but she was firm in her refusal. "Papa needs all the help he can get right now. Besides, you girls haven't finished with the root-crop. There is a kettle of beans on the stove so you won't have to cook lunch. I'll be back as soon as I can."

The sun was going down when she returned. We were waiting for her with a dozen questions. "What's she like Mama? Is she an old maid? Is she really young and pretty?"

Mama answered all of them at once. "If she's an old maid she's the prettiest one I ever saw. And a real lady, too. But I've an idea she can be stern if necessary, judging by the way she handled old Seth Arnold, the baggageman."

Papa seemed as interested as we were.

Mr. Arnold, Mama said, had insisted there were only four pieces of luggage for Miss Engles. She assured him there were five and asked him to please look again. He went back to the baggage car but returned empty handed.

"There ain't nothin' more in there, Miss," he grumbled, "and I cain't hold up the train all day. Are ye sure ye had five suitcases?"

"I'm very sure. And I'm afraid you are going to *have* to hold

30

the train until I find the missing one," she said. And with that she picked up her long skirt and climbed back onto the train. In a few minutes she appeared with the missing suitcase.

"Thank you very much, sir, for holding the train." She smiled sweetly at the old man.

"Seth was so flustered he dropped his hat and walked right over it without noticing," Mama said. "She certainly made a life-long friend of him. I'm sure he expected her to snap his head off. Most women probably would have. It seems the suitcase was there in plain sight all the time. Poor old Seth! His eyes aren't very sharp these days."

Miss Julia Engles was introduced to the community at Literary Society on Friday. A special program had been quickly arranged. Mr. Evans would give a "reading," Mrs. Phillips would play a "classic" piano composition, and Nellie Hughes would sing "Beautiful Dreamer" which everyone liked. There would be other recitations of favorite poems. For amusement, Aunt Hilda had been persuaded to repeat the story about "Old Mrs. Schmidt and the stubborn red pig," which always made everyone laugh so hard they cried.

Every seat in Goldenrod schoolhouse except those reserved by Mr. Hughes, was filled early on Friday night. While we waited for them and Miss Engles the room buzzed with whispers and laughter. Suddenly the whispering stopped and all heads turned toward the door.

I wasn't the only one to catch my breath. Miss Engles was beautiful! Her hair was as yellow as Aunt Hilda's and it was done up in a high pompadour under a small green velvet hat with feathery plumes that danced when she walked. She was as tall as Mama and very slender. Her dress was green, like her hat, and it had a long skirt with a bustle of green moire ribbon. Mrs. Hughes ushered her to the seats reserved for them next to Mr. Evans. He stood up and smiled as Mrs. Hughes whispered an introduction. Then Mrs. Phillips played the National Anthem and everyone stood up and sang.

As soon as the room was quiet again Mr. Hughes stepped to the desk and faced the audience. "I'm pleased to see a full house tonight, neighbors. And don't any of you start worrying about me making a long speech. But I would like to remind you, if you need reminding, that it was three years ago the Goldenrod School was finished. We've come a long way since then, and we owe a great deal to the fine woman who brought education to our children — Mrs. Elmer Phillips." There was spontaneous applause. "As you know, Mrs. Phillips is going to retire from teaching, but we are happy that she will continue to be a part of our community, our friend and neighbor." More applause. "And now it gives we great pleasure, Ladies and Gentlemen, to introduce to you our new teacher from St. Louis, Miss Julia Engles."

She stood up. Everyone applauded as Mr. Hughes took her hand and led her to the front of the room. She waited, smiling, until the applause quieted. Her voice was soft but her words were distinct.

"Thank you, Mr. Hughes. Thank you all for this warm welcome. I know it is not possible to take Mrs. Phillips' place here, but I shall try to make a place for myself in your fine community and in your hearts. Your confidence in selecting me to teach your children makes me very proud, indeed. With your help and advice I shall do my best to prove worthy of that honor and your trust."

The burst of applause that followed could leave no doubt in her mind how everyone felt toward her.

Mr. Hughes took the floor again as soon as she was seated. "And now, before we start the delightful program which awaits us, I should like to make a few announcements." He read several concerning events of interest to the community, then turned the meeting over to Mama who was Chairwoman. The program began. Afterwards, as usual, the seats were pushed back to make room for dancing. Mama brought Miss Engles to where we were waiting with Papa and Aunt Hilda and Uncle Ethan, and introduced her to each of us. Close up, she was even prettier, I thought. I saw now that her eyes were dark, her smile warm. Later, watching her dancing with one partner after another, it seemed the grown up men were more interested in our new teacher than they were supposed to be. Even Mr. Evans. When he put his arm about her waist for a waltz I wanted to cry.

On the way home Papa said, "She's sure a good-looker, Molly. I'll bet there won't be an empty seat in the schoolhouse on Monday."

Mama laughed. "Just so you *men* don't decide to go back to school!"

Monday morning and school were farthest from my thoughts at that moment. I was thinking that tomorrow was Saturday and I would see the one I loved. And for a while we would be alone in a world that belonged only to us.

# CHAPTER III
## 1894

Saturday was a perfect Indian Summer day. A soft haze hung over the browning prairies where cattle grazed in the sun's mellow warmth. A flock of noisy blackbirds fluttered greedily about. Hawks sailed high against the smoky-blue sky. In the meadows larks and bob-o-links added their songs to the new day.

I turned Midnight onto the familiar prairie path toward Mr. Evans' farm. The reins lay loosely about the saddle horn. She knew the way. The basket, with butter and eggs and a packet of freshly-baked cookies, rested safely on the saddle in front of me. On top of it, carefully wrapped, was the book I had just finished.

My thoughts fell into an even rhythm with Midnight's footsteps. This was the special day I had waited for all week. I thought of what I would say about the book I'd finished, trying to shape my comments. I wanted him to be proud of how well I understood it. Most of all I wanted him to talk with me as a grownup, not as if I were a child with special talents. I remembered the way he had looked at Miss Engles while they were dancing. A shadow fell across the morning. Would he be different today? Would her coming here make a difference between us? The possibility was so disturbing I urged Midnight to a gallop, forgetting about the eggs.

He was waiting on the steps when I rode in. My heart leaped at sight of him and his welcoming smile. Nothing had changed!

He called to me, coming down the steps. "Good morning, Ann! And what a glorious morning it is. These Indian Summer days are worthy of a symphony."

He took the basket and set it on the ground while he helped me down and tied Midnight in the shade and watered her. Then we went inside. The tea-kettle steamed on the back of the stove. There were sandwiches on a tray on the kitchen table and he had set out the china cups he told me he had brought from England. He *had* anticipated my coming! He took my sunbonnet and hung it on a peg behind the kitchen door.

"I thought you would be hungry after your ride. The sand-

34

wiches aren't very elegant, I'm afraid, but they will be filling."
He set about making the tea.

"Mama sent you some sugar cookies, too."

"Fine! And most thoughtful of her. We shall have some of
them with our tea." He added several to the sandwich plate and
picked up the tray. I walked ahead of him into the library. This
was our room!

We sat in the big brocaded chairs and sipped tea and ate
sandwiches and cookies, and talked. This was the fulfillment of
all I had waited for. He told me about his life in New York
at the University, and of the years he had spent in England
studying and roaming the historic countryside. We talked about
the books he wanted me to read—books he had cherished when
he was my age — and why they had meant so much to him.

And all the time my heart was singing. *Nothing has changed!
Nothing has changed.*

Later, as he scanned the bookcases to find the right book for
me, he paused suddenly. "We've forgotten school starts on
Monday. Will you have time for more outside reading now,
Ann?"

"Oh, yes, Mr. Evans. School work is easy for me." I couldn't
bear the thought of missing our Saturday talks.

He seemed to study me for a moment, "Yes, my dear, I'm
sure it is. Learning probably will always be easy for you. You
have the rare gift of *wanting* to know, to understand." He
turned back to the bookcase. "Well, what shall it be? You've
read most of Dickens and Thackery and several of Scott's novels.
Let's see if we can find something different."

He walked slowly along the shelf and presently took from it
a slender volume. For a moment he stood turning the pages
almost lovingly. "Do you enjoy poetry, Ann?"

"Oh, very much, Mr. Evans. Mama often reads poetry aloud
to all of us when we've finished our lessons. She calls it our
reward."

"You must not confuse poetry with verse," he said solemnly.
"There is quite a difference, you know. Verse may be excellent
*as* verse, but that does not make it poetry. Each has its own
distinguishing meter and style, better understood perhaps as
measures of rhythm." He stopped suddenly and laughed. "There
I go, talking like a professor again. Please forgive me!"

"Oh, no you weren't Mr. Evans. Please go on."

"Very well, my dear. What I wanted to say is that I believe you will appreciate fine poetry, understand it better than most. I am strongly convinced that youth is the proper time for poetry. We tend to lose our sensitivity to its nuances as we grow older. There are a great many books of fine poetry I should like you to read. Tennyson, Byron, Wordsworth, and of course some by both the Brownings. I thought you might begin with this little volume by Elizabeth Barrett Browning, *Sonnets from the Portuguese*. It is one of my favorites."

I took the book from him. It was bound in rich red leather with gold lettering. "Thank you," I said, finding no words for what was in my heart.

He told me then that Elizabeth was the wife of Robert Browning, one of the great poets of our time; that she also became a great poet and was more widely known, perhaps, than her husband largely because of the book he wanted me to read.

"Their marriage was one of the memorable stories in English history. Mrs. Browning expressed that devotion most tenderly in her Sonnets. However, that alone is not my reason for wanting you to read this little book. I'm sure you will enjoy it, but I'd like you to study the rhythm and compelling word power. There is no better way, Ann, to learn the effective use of words than by the study of fine poetry."

Inspired by these words and that he *was* treating me like a grown up, I confessed that it was my ambition one day to become a writer.

"Splendid, my dear! Splendid! Come, let us toast that worthy ambition with another cup of tea. Besides, you've had quite enough lecture from me today. Although I can't promise not to repeat the performance from time to time. Once a professor, always a professor! Isn't that the way the saying goes?"

He sat down and filled the cups again. I didn't particularly want more tea but I was in no hurry to go.

"I'm very pleased by your 'confession', Ann. There is no finer achievement than the ability to express one's thoughts well. Later on, you must read some of Charlotte Bronte's works. I'm sure you've read most of Louisa May Alcott's novels, have you not?"

I told him I had read only *Little Women*.

"Well, there will be time for many books, my dear, when you

have finished school. I'm sure you're looking forward to opening day on Monday, aren't you?"

"Yes, I like school, but my sisters don't."

"That's unfortunate. I'm afraid few teachers seem able to make learning the adventure that it truly it. A fine teacher is all too rare." He smiled suddenly. "I think we may have found one of these in Miss Engles. She impressed me as quite dedicated to helping young people with learning. I imagine there will be a roomful of eager pupils on Monday. Miss Engles is a very attractive young lady."

For a moment I resented her intrusion into our special day. Then I think I was ashamed of my own selfishness. This day had been too wonderful to be unhappy about anything. Besides, Miss Engles was very pretty.

"Yes," I said. "Mama and Papa were also impressed. Mama says she is sure to be the best teacher we could have found."

"Your mother is a most remarkable woman, Ann. Be sure to thank her for agreeing with me! *And* for these delicious cookies."

I knew it was time to go. He brought my bonnet and walked with me to where Midnight was tied up, and helped me to mount.

"I have enjoyed our visit immensely, Ann. Do come again soon. But I shall see you at church on Sunday, won't I?"

I assured him he would. At the gate I turned and waved, then gave Midnight her head. He *was* looking forward to seeing me on Sunday! And he had lent me a book of love poems!


School opened as scheduled on Monday. Every seat was filled. Miss Engles looked quite different in a high-necked white shirt-waist and long black skirt. She wasn't nearly as pretty as I had thought. Except maybe her hair. It *was* beautiful and I liked the way she wore it. Otherwise, I decided, she wasn't any prettier than some of the other girls in our community. Somehow this comforted me.

Before very long all of us knew Miss Engles was a good teacher as well as a pretty one. She had a way of challenging us to learn instead of making us feel we had to study. I thought of Mr. Evans' remarks on Saturday about teachers and teaching, and smiled to myself. The students were certainly *eager!* Even the most unruly boys settled down the moment she came into the room, and in several ways she challenged them to learn. But I didn't need *her* challenge. Mr. Evans had said I had a rare gift for learning!

Early in November the first snowstorm of winter swept across the prairies. A stiff north wind piled drifts high against barns and houses. Frost nipped at our fingers and toes on the way to school. Usually a heavy snowfall was all the excuse some of the students needed to miss school, but not this year. Everyone was present at roll-call. Recess was boisterous with snowballing and games, but when the bell rang we were careful to shake the snow from out coats and to wipe our feet before entering the schoolroom again.

One afternoon as we were putting away our books, Miss Engles stopped by my desk. "Would you please stay a while, Ann?

"Yes, Miss Engles." I wondered what I had done to displease her. I could think of nothing, but I waited in my seat while the room emptied. Miss Engles went outside, as usual, to see that the younger pupils were safely on their way home, and to caution them against loitering. While she was gone Vina came back to the door. "Aren't you ready yet, Ann?"

"Not quite. You kids go on. I'll catch up with you."

"All right, but don't forget we have to do the milking before dark."

From the window I could see her throwing snowballs at the boys and keeping out of their way when they chased her. Lucy wasn't so lucky. She got her face washed.

Miss Engles came back. "Thank you for waiting, Ann. I thought we might have a little talk. Come up here, please."

Still puzzled as to what I had done, I sat down beside her desk waiting for the scolding I was sure would come. She picked up a school-paper from her desk and I saw it was my composition titled *Pioneer Women*. I had worked very hard on it and thought it quite good.

"Did you have outside help with this composition, Ann?" she asked.

"No, Miss Engles."

"According to school records, you are fourteen. Is that correct?"

"I'll be fifteen next week."

She studied the paper a moment. "This is a remarkable piece of writing for one so young. I wanted to be sure it was your thinking, Ann, not influenced by someone else."

I almost sighed with relief. "Thank you, Miss Engles. I tried to write what I thought about pioneer women. My grandmother was one of them. I guess my mother, too, in a way. And they're both wonderful."

"I know your mother. She is, indeed, a very fine woman. Have you always lived in Iowa?"

"Oh, no. Papa had a farm in Illinois near Roanoke where my grandmother lives. We lived there until he bought this farm about four years ago."

"Yes, I've seen your farm. You must all be very happy here. So much open country to roam about in."

"We are now. But none of us wanted to come so far west. We came because of Papa's pioneering spirit. Mama says that is important to a man, and women have to see they keep it."

"Do you agree with that?"

I hesitated. "Yes, in a way, I guess. But I think women have to have it, too. That is what I tried to say in my composition. I don't think it is fair for men to get all the credit for everything."

Miss Engles laughed. "I agree with that whole-heartedly! We women have to stick together." She became serious again. "You've written a fine composition, Ann. Your mother has taught you well. You are fortunate. I lost my mother when I was seven."

I said how sorry I was. She told me then about the aunt who had taken care of her until she finished college and found a teaching position. "She was very good to me. We had wonderful times together. I still miss her very much." She seemed to come back from a place of memories. "Well, I think we had better be getting home. We have quite a distance to walk and it gets dark early these days." She put my composition in her desk and got up.

Wrapped against the cold we went outside. I waited on the steps while she locked the door, then she took my arm and walked with me down the slippery path. At the main road we separated.

All the way home I thought about the kind things she had said. If I had been a good student before, now I was determined to be the best. Maybe I *could* become a famous writer if I worked very hard. I'd go away to school in St. Louis, or Boston, or maybe New York and wear beautiful clothes and everyone would be very proud of me when I came home on vacations. And I wanted to look just like Miss Engles! Oh, I could never be as pretty as she was but I *could* make the most of my looks.

For weeks afterwards, when Vina or Lucy wasn't around to make fun of me, I'd try fixing my hair the way she fixed hers. And once when Mama had gone to town and I knew Vina and Lucy were far enough away from the house, I dressed up in one of Mama's long dresses and practiced walking elegantly, the way Miss Engles did. Oh, why did it take so long to grow up?

During these weeks of new ambition I had not forgotten my secret love. I did not tell anyone about the book of poetry he had lent me; I kept it hidden in my dresser drawer, at the very bottom where Vina wasn't likely to find it. I had read it once, but I wanted to read it again and again before I returned it. The first reading had been in secret. I had taken the book with me that Saturday afternoon when I went to bring the cows from pasture. The sun was still warm. In the buffalo hollows there was almost no wind, and the cows were in no hurry to get home. Lost in the beauty of the words, I read on and on. It was dusk when I came to the end of the book. Filled with a kind of wonderful sadness, I lay down in the thick grass and cried, not knowing why.

The next Saturday Mama took the produce to him on her way to town. But until the weather turned colder, I took the book with me whenever I was sure I would be alone, re-reading parts of it over and over.

Winter closed in with more frequent and severe snowstorms. My visits to Mr. Evans were no longer possible. Once a week, when the weather was suitable, he came to our place for his supplies. Usually I was in school at the time. Now I saw him rarely except at church and Literary Society. It was not the same.

I longed for spring and the return of our treasured hours in his library. I still had the book of poems. It had snowed hard the day I'd planned to return it, and Mama wouldn't let me go. Just knowing it was there, hidden in my dresser, gave me a warm and wonderful feeling. It was a kind of link between us, I thought, and the waiting for spring became less difficult.

One evening toward the end of November, while we were having supper, there was a knock on the door. The heavy snowfall that day made traveling hazardous. We wondered who would be out at this time of night. Papa answered the knock, and quickly swung the door wider. "Come in, Jed. Come in. What are . . . ."

Jed didn't take his coat off. He said he had been to town for the doctor and stopped by for Mama. Elsie's time had come. Mama quickly packed a small valise and went with him. She did not return that night. But the next night when we returned from school she was home.

"Is Elsie all right, Mama?" I asked for all of us.

"Elsie is fine. She has a healthy little boy."

"When can we see him? When?" Lucy pleaded.

"Soon. When Elsie is up and around and the weather is better."

Elsie named him David Charles, but he was "little Davey" to all of us. After the christening Papa handed out cigars as if *he* was the baby's father, and bragged about "my grandson". Mama was just as proud to be a grandmother but she didn't talk much about it. Mama was a "doer" not a "talker". She spent as much time as possible with Elsie, and her hands were never idle at home. The moment supper was over she got out her sewing basket. Always she was making something for Davey.

Gradually our lives settled into a normal pattern once more. Papa found some reason to stop by the Miller farm several times every week. If Elsie still felt resentment toward him for past harshness, his devotion to little Davey at least softened it.

Christmas that year was especially festive. Everything centered around Davey. Papa came home from town a few days before Christmas loaded with presents for the boy. Mama examined them and smiled.

"Goodness gracious, Sam! Davey's not a month old yet. These things are for a five-year-old boy, not a baby."

Papa looked a little confused for a minute. "He'll grow up fast in this country. Kids do. Why, in no time at all he'll be dragging that sled every place. It's a real fine one, Molly. Nothing is too good for our grandson!"

Mama agreed with that. Nevertheless she went right on knitting sweaters and little socks and making clothes for him.

The tree Papa had brought from town along with the sled and toys, was set up in the parlor. We trimmed it with the usual garlands of popcorn and red berries and colored paper chains we had made ourselves, and spread cotton snow on the floor beneath its thick branches. The day before Christmas Mama baked and cooked everything she could prepare in advance. There would be a houseful of company on Christmas Day. I hoped Mama had invited Mr. Evans but when I asked her about it she said he and Rev. Pritchard were going to the Hugheses for Christmas dinner. That was where Miss Engles lived.

But on Christmas Day when the presents were distributed, I knew he had not forgotten me. He had sent me a beautiful book of poems by William Wordsworth, inscribed, "To my dear friend, Ann."

# CHAPTER IV
# 1895

The New Year of 1895 came in with a blizzard which swept across the open prairie on a forty-mile wind. In moments the windbreak, the barn, orchards, even the windmill, were blotted from sight. It beat relentlessly against the window panes. Rims of white formed on the sills. Fine snow drifted in beneath the kitchen door. The house shook as if pushed about by giant hands. Lamps flickered and blackened the chimneys.

Mama brought gunnysacks from the storeroom off the kitchen and stuffed them in the crack at the bottom of the door. She piled more coal into the range until the lids were cherry red. We ate our breakfast listening to the howling wind, and thinking about the New Year dance tonight at the schoolhouse, which no one could get to. Papa couldn't even get to the barn to feed the stock.

"Why couldn't the old storm wait one more day?" Vina grumbled. She rarely complained about anything, but she had planned to wear the new dress Aunt Hilda had given her for Christmas. I knew how disappointed she was. I was disappointed too, for a different reason. I wanted to see Mr. Evans to thank him for the book he'd given me. I had read some of it. Much of it I didn't understand but I'd have to wait until I could visit him again to discuss it.

Mama put another stack of pancakes on Papa's plate before she answered Vina's complaint. "Old man winter doesn't wait for anyone, honey. But the storm will pass. You'll have plenty of chances to wear your new dress."

The storm didn't pass. Not right away. For three days the winds roared and shrieked and thick clouds of snow blotted out the world. It gave me a scary feeling, as if we were the only people left, all others had been buried in snowdrifts or blown away.

Papa had not waited for the storm to pass. About noon on the first day he said, "Looks like it's not going to let up. I've got to see to the stock."

Mama brought two thick sweaters and his heavy storm coat. He put on a cap with fur earlaps and wrapped a woolen scarf over his head and around his throat, and pulled on his boots. Vina and I started to put on our leggings and overshoes.

"Where do you kids think you're going?" Papa asked.

"To help you," I said.

He laughed. "In this blizzard? Those drifts are over your head. If you stepped into one of 'em I'd be the rest of the winter digging you out."

"Then I'd better go," Mama said. "You can't do the chores alone, not in this storm."

"It wouldn't be the first time. You keep that fire going and have a pot of hot coffee when I get back."

Papa had been quite changed for some time but this kind of consideration none of us expected. The chores, he had always insisted, were a part of farm life and easy or not they had to be done. A little cold never hurt anyone. How many times I had heard him say that! Was he still under the spell of Christmas?

Papa took the milk pails in one mittened hand. The other had to be free to hold onto the rope stretched between the house and barn. He opened the door just enough to squeeze through and stepped outside. A blast of wind swept in a little pile of snow before Mama could close it. She pushed the gunnysacks back against the door and swept up the snow before she went on fixing New Year's dinner. The ham had been baking since before we girls were up. It would have been taken to the party at the schoolhouse had we been able to go. Now she put wedges of sweet potatoes into the roasting pan to brown in the rich dippings, stirred up a big batch of baking powder biscuits.

"See if there's a jar of plum butter in the buttery Ann. It's Papa's favorite. And open that jar of spiced apples , too. We'll have them with the cake."

Dinner was everything Papa liked. The storm still showed no signs of letting up. It was a long day. Vina helped Lucy make dresses for her doll from material they found in Mama's scrap bag. Mae played with her blocks on a rug spread beside the stove. Mama kept busy with mending, and Papa read last week's newspaper. I read the book Mr. Evans had given me and for a while forgot the storm.

Night came. A cold grey blanket covered the land.

In the afternoon of the third day the winds died down but the snow continued. We wiped frost from the kitchen window.

Through a curtain of snow we could dimly see the effects of the three-day storm. The trees in the windbreak bent under mounds of snow. Huge drifts, half as tall as the trees themselves, banked their trunks. Branches of cottonwood and fruit trees were crusted with snow and ice. Occasionally a gust of wind swept through them. We could hear the groaning and cracking all the way to the house. Clumps of gooseberry and blackberry bushes along the back fence looked like an army of snowmen.

At last the winds blew themselves out. The snowing stopped. But the bitter cold remained, the skies grey and threatening, all through January. Papa said it was too cold to snow. At least we could be thankul for that. We had had more than enough snow for one winter. It lay in deep billowing waves as far as the eye could see, an endless expanse of white except where the road cut a grey gash across it. Papa took us to and from school in the bobsled. A couple of times he went to town for supplies and brought back reports from the hardware store for Mama's examination.

"Things are sure quiet in town. Not much business except at Bruckners. Folks have to eat, I guess, blizzard or not." He gave Mama the reports and took off his coat and overshoes and warmed his hands over the range.

"Well, we can't complain," Mama said. "We had a good year, with the crops and profits from the hardware store." She got up and poured two cups of coffee and sat down again. "I've been thinking, Sam . . . . ."

Papa gave her a worried look. "I don't like the sound of that. What are you up to now, Molly?"

"Nothing we can't handle. It's about the addition to the house. We've been putting that off long enough. We should get it built this spring. The girls are getting too big to be crowded into one bedroom. And we need a larger parlor. It's time they had music lessons and our parlor is too small for an organ."

Papa almost choked on his coffee. "Have you lost your senses, Molly! Just because we've got a little money in the bank's no reason to start spending it on tomfool gimcracks. I've still got the rest of the mortgage to pay. Or have you forgotten there's a payment due in March?"

"No, Sam. You can meet that out of the farm money. I intend to pay for the addition to the house and the organ out of profits from my investments."

"Your profits! Farm or hardware store or rentals, they're all one and the same."

"Not exactly, Sam. The money in the bank is in three accounts. Farm, hardware store, and rental income. You handle the money in the farm account. The other two accounts I handle. We've been doing it this way for the past year, Sam. It has proved satisfactory, don't you agree?"

"Satisfactory, my eye! You're my wife, or have you forgotten that? What's your is mine."

Mama remained calm. "In a way that's true. And I'm proud to be your wife, Sam. You must know that. And the money from my investments *is* used for the benefit of all of us as a family, as it should be. There was a time, if you'll remember, when we were in danger of losing everything."

"A man makes mistakes sometimes," Papa said stubbornly.

"The important thing is we didn't lose the farm or the hardware store. We have prospered. Now it seems to me we should use some of that prosperity to better our lives. We can manage the mortgage payment and the addition to the house. And when we're ready for it, an organ."

Papa finished his coffee and got up and put on his coat and overshoes. "All right, Molly. *You're* wearing the pants but I've got chores to do!" He went out, closing the door without slamming it.

We helped Mama get supper on the table. It was ready when he came in with the brimming milk pails crusted with thin ice. He seemed to have left his temper at the barn or lost it in a snowdrift.

"Add a few eggs to that, Molly, and we'll have ice-cream for supper." He set the pails on the drainboard.

I wondered what had made him change so quickly. Maybe it was simply that he couldn't bear for anyone to be right about anything but himself. When he knew Mama was right about something he couldn't just say so, he had to blow off steam or storm around a while before he admitted it. Even then he tried to make it appear he had given in only to keep peace in the family.

Nothing more was said about the addition to the house that night. After supper, while we girls were studying, Mama played a game of dominoes with him. Papa won. I had an idea Mama had planned it that way. She popped a big bowl of corn and brought a bowl of apples from the buttery. We stayed up until almost nine o'clock.

We undressed by the kitchen range and put on our outing-flannel night-gowns, then scurried up the stairs and jumped into bed. Our toes reached for the heated bricks Mama had put there while we got ready for bed. Gradually our teeth stopped chattering. Vina and I talked in whispers about the organ Mama was going to buy.

"Won't it take a long time to learn to play it?" Vina asked.

"Maybe not, if we practice every day."

"Who wants to do that? I'd rather ride Golden, or play bean-bag."

"You'll change your mind when you see the new organ. And we're going to have a new parlor, too. You heard what Mama said. And our very own room. I hope we get the new one. I know just the kind of curtains I want."

Vina was quiet a moment. "Yeah! I didn't think about that. I guess we really *are* rich, aren't we?"

February continued cold with mostly leaden skies. Occasionally the clouds parted spreading thin sunshine without warmth over snowy fields. Then as suddenly, greyness closed in again and light feathery snow fell steadily for the rest of the day. By nightfall the temperature usually dropped to fifteen below, sometimes colder. New snow became another layer of ice. Already the deep snows of January were frozen hard enough to hold up the bobsled and a team of horses.

Bundled against the stinging cold we went about our daily lives. Church services were resumed. The Literary Society met that Friday for the first time since the blizzard. Mr. Evans traveled about now in a bright new bobsled and took Miss Engles home from every community gathering. This almost broke my heart. As much as I liked her I couldn't help being jealous he was spending time with her while I was snow-bound. I prayed for an early spring but the winter seemed endless.

Early in March Chinook winds began to melt the snow. Little

brown hillocks emerged in fields and pastures. By the middle of March buffalo-wallows and ditches along roadsides brimmed with brown water. Mud, thick and sticky, was everywhere. We waded through it to and from school and to help with the chores. With the deep snowdrifts gone, Papa no longer did the chores alone. Often we would have welcomed the return of winter. Then I would remember how eagerly I had waited for spring and was always glad when it finally arrived.

Winter did not return that year. The days continued unseasonably warm with clear skies. Evenings, great flocks of wild geese winged northward in the high, blue dusk, their cries drifting slowly down. Spring had come again to the prairies.

March brought some exciting news. Grandma was coming for a visit. She had written Mama, "I'm eager to see all of you, and my first great-grandchild." She would arrive the third of April on the afternoon train.

Now there was a bustle of activity. Carpets came up, straw ticks were emptied and refilled with fresh straw. Throughout the house was a pervading odor of oil and kerosene Mama used to clean and polish furniture. I had no chance to visit Mr. Evans, or even much time to think about him.

Excitement always seemed to come in twos and threes. A few days after Grandma's letter had arrived, Aunt Hilda stopped by to tell us Mr. and Mrs. Phillips had a ten-pound boy. They had named him Robert Ethan, and the christening was to be held the first Sunday in April. Grandma would be here in time for it.

We weren't really surprised when we met Grandma's train to find Uncle Phil with her. Papa had been too busy with spring plowing to drive us to town to meet the train. In spite of still muddy roads Mama hitched the greys to the surrey and took all of us with her. Elmer's buggy was tied to the hitching rail in front of the station when we arrived.

Grandma stepped off the train and gathered us, one by one, into her arms. She hadn't changed a bit, except now she wore a stylish dress and hat. I'd almost never seen her in anything but a housedress and apron before, and I thought how grand she looked. But whatever she wore she was still the nicest Grandma in the whole world.

Uncle Phil shook hands with Mama. "How are you, Molly? You look as blooming as a spring flower. This country sure agrees with you." He hugged each of us girls and told us how pretty we'd grown. "How's Sam doing?"

"We're all fine, Phil. Sam was too busy with planting to come with us today. It's good to see you. And congratulations, Grandpa."

Uncle Phil chuckled. "Isn't that something! I'd be the biggest liar in Iowa if I didn't admit I'm about to burst with pride. Did you know they named him after me?"

"You and Uncle Ethan," Vina blurted.

"Can't complain about that. He must be a fine man if Elmer gave his name to my grandson. I'm anxious to meet him."

"You will, Pa," Elmer said. "But right now I'm taking all of you to Jason's Ice Cream Parlor to celebrate. I can't offer the women cigars, can I?"

"May we go Mama?" Lucy pleaded.

Mama shook her head. "We'd like to celebrate with you, Elmer, and you're kind to invite us. But Grandma and your father have had a long tiring trip. And Sam will be expecting us. Maybe we'd better save the celebration until later."

"Molly's right, son," Uncle Phil agreed. "I'm a lot more interested in seeing my grandson than in ice cream." He turned to Mama. "But there's no reason the kids can't have some candy, is there?"

Mama said it was all right. We went with Elmer to Jason's.

Supper that night was a feast. Papa was in a jovial mood and talked endlessly about *his* grandson, what a remarkable boy he was. "Wait 'til you see him, Mother Dauber. Smart as a new whip. Knows me the minute I step into the house."

Later, when Papa went outside to get more coal, Grandma said, "Sam's changed, Molly. Iowa life seems to have tempered him. He's more like the man you married."

"I guess we have all changed a good deal since Grandpa died. I wish he could be here to see how much the money he left me has helped. Life isn't so hard now. Sometimes I think we have more than our share of the good things."

"No more than you deserve, dear. I'm sure that is what your father had in mind when he left the money to you. He would be pleased with the way you've used it."

Papa came back with the coal and an armful of kindling. "Looks like it's going to be a fine day tomorrow. Not a cloud in the sky. We'll drive over to Elsie's first thing after breakfast."

Mama made a bed on the parlor floor for Lucy and Mae. Grandma would have their bed. Long after we girls were in bed, Mama and Papa and Grandma sat in the kitchen, talking. We could hear their voices but we couldn't make out much they were saying. Once in a while Papa's voice got a little louder but he didn't sound angry, just excited. I supposed they were talking about the hardware store and the buildings Mama had bought. Or the addition to the house and the organ Mama was going to buy. We must have fallen asleep listening. I didn't hear Grandma come upstairs to bed.

With so much other excitement in our lives, it was the end of April before I was permitted to ride over to see Mr. Evans. I was sure things would be different, it had been so long since I had seen him alone. But nothing had changed. He came out to meet me, watered and tied up Midnight and took the basket I carried, and walked arm-in-arm with me back to the house. We had tea in the library. I returned the book of poetry I had kept so long, and for a while we talked about it. Then he showed me the new books he had received from his friends in the East as Christmas gifts. And finally we discussed my treasured book of Wordsworth's poems which he had given me for Christmas.

I told him I loved the poems but there were many I did not fully understand.

"I did not expect you would understand all of it at first reading, Ann. Such books are for re-reading. Wisdom and prophecy abound in Wordsworth's poetry, which you are still too young to understand. The important point now is that you *feel* their beauty and rhythm and catch glimpses of his wisdom which inspire you to reach out, stretch your mind, as it were. Note how, with a word or a line, the poet lifts you from despair to joyousness, lets you share for that fragment of time his own sublime emotions."

He got up and walked about the room reciting passages to illustrate what he had said. I marveled that he knew so many of them by heart.

Riding home across the prairie I knew that this day was one

to treasure. But I could not know then how many seeds of wisdom and understanding he had planted in my eager mind.

All too soon Grandma and Uncle Phil returned to their homes. Our lives settled once more into familiar routines. Plowing and planting, weeding and cultivating. Most of these tasks were now done by Papa and Cyrus Crump. But the gardens were still our responsibility, and the orchards to some extent. Mama resumed her weekly trips to town for supplies and to check hardware accounts with Donald Matthews. Nights we studied our lessons in the warm glow of lamplight and checked off the days until school would be out for the summer.

One Friday evening in early May Papa said, "I'll go into town with you tomorrow, Molly. Thought we'd see about lumber for the addition." He glanced at Mama, a twinkle in his eyes. "Unless you want to *select* it as well as pay for it."

Mama smiled. "I think you'd better come along."

Soon the sound of hammers and saws filled the mornings and greeted us on our return from school. By the end of the month the new rooms were ready to move into. Mama's new parlor was considerably larger than the old one. Somehow even the furniture looked much grander. The upstairs part of the addition was big enough to divide into two more bedrooms, one for Mama and Papa, and one for Vina and me. The old parlor became the sitting-room. At last Mama had a sitting-room, parlor *and* dining-room.

The following week Mama and Papa went to town in the big farm wagon, and brought back new furniture for their bedroom and the dining-room. There was also a big wooden crate which contained the organ Mama had ordered weeks ago. It was an exciting and busy day. There were braided rag carpets for the new bedroom and dining-room, put down with generous paddings of straw the night before. Papa and Cyrus carried in the new furniture. How beautiful it was! A double bed and a dresser with mirror attached, commodes and chests of drawers, a flowered china lamp with pitcher and bowl to match. There was a big round dark-oak table for the dining-room and six chairs with red plush seats, and a sideboard with a beveled mirror across the back.

Finally the organ was uncrated and carried in. It was even

more beautiful than I had dreamed it could be. The dark wood which Mama said was mahogany shone like a mirror. The stool had a green-velvet seat. As soon as everything was in place, Mama sat down at the organ and played her favorite hymn, *The Great Physician* . . . . .

Even Papa agreed that such a grand house called for a "housewarming". It was set for the following Saturday. All day Friday Mama prepared the food. Bright and early Saturday morning the new dining table was extended with all its extra "leaves" and spread with Mama's best tablecloth. Vina and Lucy and I made sure there wasn't a speck of dust on the furniture. Shortly after noon the guests began to arrive. Mr. Evans brought Miss Engles in his new buggy. Nellie Hughes, pretty as a picture in a grown up dress, came with Rev. Pritchard. The Millers came with Elsie and Jed and little Davey. Elmer and Nora Phillips with little Bobbie, the Rogers family, the Gruders, the Jenkins, the McCavitys and the Setons. The house was filled, spilling over into the front yard where Papa had set up the croquet set. "Refreshments" were served buffet-style. Everyone filled a plate and carried it to the table, or outside where they could watch the game. Afterwards the young people gathered around the organ. Nora Phillips played our favorite songs and everyone joined in the singing.

It was the nicest party we had ever had. Mama smiled proudly when the neighbors complimented her on the lovely home, especially the new organ.

"I'd like Ann and Vina to have music lessons, Nora, if you can manage the time. Lucy and Mae can wait until next year."

"I'm sure I can manage. If both girls come at the same time, One can look after Bobbie while the other is having her lesson. How does that sound, girls?"

Lessons would start next month. Vina wasn't very happy about it. "Just when it's warm enough to enjoy riding we have to stay in and practice."

"Not all day, silly."

I could scarcely wait for the lessons to begin. With books *and* music, and our beautiful new home there seemed nothing more to wish for. But later, as I watched Mr. Evans and Miss Engles drive away together I changed my mind.

# CHAPTER V
## 1895

The close of school the end of May each year was a significant time. For most pupils, especially the older boys, it did not mean vacation. There was farm work awaiting them, long sweaty days in the fields under a sun that burned hotly in a cloudless sky day after day. But there was a sense of freedom too in the change from schoolroom to open fields. The labors of the week were rewarded by Saturday night square-dancing under the stars, Sunday picnics, and buggy rides in the moonlight with the girl or boy of your choice.

This year the end of school held for us a two-fold freedom. Papa no longer required us to work in the fields. There were hired men now to do cultivating and haying, to shock wheat and oat crops and gather wagon loads of corn. We tended the vegetable garden and helped pick fruit as it ripened, and with its canning. Driving the cows to pasture each morning was more fun than work. We brought them in at night, too, but Papa and one of the hands did the milking.

There was time now for our music lessons, for reading, and for long rides. Several times Vina and I had ridden all the way to the little clump of trees I had seen that first snowy morning from Uncle Ethan's bobsled. There wasn't a stream as I'd thought there might be, but it was cool under the big cottonwoods and the grass was tall and soft. We let our horses graze while we stretched out on the grass and dreamed and talked. "It sure is a lot nicer than it used to be," Vina remarked. I certainly agreed with that.

I looked forward each week to our music lessons. I didn't even mind the two hours of practice Mama insisted upon every day after Papa had left for the fields. But the most exciting time for me still was Saturday and my visits with Mr. Evans. I knew he drove Miss Engles to church and Literary Society and other community gatherings, but I told myself that was out of courtesy. I couldn't bear to think it might be more than that. Saturdays, alone with him in his library, having tea and talking of many things, I was sure he cared as deeply for me as I did for him. These hours belonged only to us.

One Saturday, shortly after school was out, Midnight and I took the path across the pasture to Mr. Evans farm. A warm gentle wind rippled the grass. The sky was cloudless blue. And my heart sang. Today was a very special day. It was his birthday and I was taking him a cake Mama had baked especially for him. I held Midnight to a slow pace to make sure the creamy white cocoanut icing didn't get smeared. The cake would be a surprise. He didn't know I knew today was his birthday. At least I was sure he wouldn't remember mentioning it last summer, or think I would remember.

It was almost noon when we arrived. Mr. Evans was not at the gate to greet me as usual. My heart sank. What if he weren't at home? Surely he wouldn't forget it was Saturday! Perhaps something had taken him away unexpectedly and he'd left a note for me. I urged Midnight to the hitching post under the cottonwood tree, and was trying to get down without damaging the cake or breaking the eggs, when I heard the screen door open.

"Good morning, Ann. I didn't hear you ride in." He hurried down the steps and took the basket and the cake box, and helped me down.

"Be careful with the box, please. It's something special for you."

"Now what have you been up to, young lady?"

"You'll see! It's a surprise."

At the back porch steps he paused. "We have a guest today, Ann. Miss Engles is having tea with us. She's waiting in the library."

The world seemed to spin around me. My feet seemed too heavy to lift. Somehow I got up the steps and into the kitchen. He set the cake box on the table beside the basket of eggs and butter, and came to take my bonnet.

I wanted to cry out, "Why! Oh, why today of all days?" But I forced a smile and untied my bonnet and gave it to him. He hung it on the peg behind the kitchen door. Watching him do these things he had done a dozen times on my visits here, today seemed strange. How *could* he have invited someone else to share *our* day? My wonderful surprise was spoiled.

"Come," he said, taking my arm. "You two can talk while I prepare the tea."

He hadn't even opened the box! Wasn't he interested in my surprise? Reluctantly I went with him into the library, knowing it would not be the same—that never again *could* it be the same, our place, our special private world.

"Hello, Ann! How nice to see you!" She came and hugged me and regarded me with a smile. "You get prettier very day. And I honestly believe you've grown an inch at least this past year."

Compliments always embarrassed me, and right now I didn't appreciate them from her. But I said "Thank you, Miss Engles", and waited to see which chair she would take. Not *my* chair, oh, please, not that one!

Mr. Evans took each of us by the arm and led us to the divan. "You girls catch up with local gossip. Ann brought me a surprise package and I can't wait a moment longer to open it." He left us alone.

Silence hung between us for a moment. I was embarrassed and tongue-tied. And suddenly I felt very drab and awkward. She was so absolutely beautiful! It wasn't fair! She wore a green dotted swiss dress with very short sleeves and low neck. Her hair was a cluster of golden curls on top of her head. When she smiled at me I just wanted to die. If she smiled that way at Mr. Evans he'd surely fall in love with her and I'd never see him again alone.

"Isn't this a beautiful room?" she said, glancing about. "So many wonderful books. James tells me you've read a great many of the classics this past year."

How dare she call him by his first name as if he belonged to her!

I agreed the room was very beautiful. I wanted to tell her, too, it was *our room,* and send her away. Instead I said politely, "Yes, I love books. Mr. Evans has been very kind to lend me many of his. He says it will take me a long time to read all the books he wants me to read."

"Wanting to read is a gift in itself, Ann. It saddens me so many young people today seem to prefer livelier recreation. If only they knew how much they are missing." She turned to me and smiled. "I'm very happy *you* aren't missing that enchanting world, my dear."

Mr. Evans came in with the tea tray. Today it was a large

silver tray, big enough to hold the tea service and a cake plate. "Just *see* what Ann brought, Julia! My favorite kind of cake." He set the tray down and came and kissed me on the forehead. "Thank you, my dear! Thank you very much. It's a magnificent cake, indeed."

"Happy birthday, Mr. Evans!" I cried.

His surprise was my reward. "Ann! How did you know that?"

Miss Engles broke in. "James, you didn't tell me this was to be a birthday party."

"I didn't know it was, until now. How *did* you know, Ann?"

I laughed. "You told me yourself. Last year at the Fourth of July picnic, remember? You said you were born a month too soon for the picnic to be in your honor. I figured it out and Mama baked the cake for you this morning."

"I'm flattered, Ann. Imagine your remembering that for a whole year."

I wanted to tell him how much more I remembered, and would always remember.

"It's been a long time since I had a birthday party," he said, "and I couldn't spend it with two lovelier ladies."

It was impossible to be angry with him when he was so happy.

With great ceremony he brought half a dozen small candles from the library table drawer and placed them on the cake.

Miss Engles laughed. "Only six, James?"

"That's exactly how old I feel today. Come, Ann. You must light the candles. The giver, you know . . ." He handed me a box of matches he kept on his desk for lighting his pipe. The tiny flames made the snowy icing glisten.

He sighed happily. "Ah, it is much too lovely to spoil! *Must* I blow them out?"

"Unless you want a waxed cocoanut icing," Miss Engles teased.

"Make a wish first!" I cried. "It will come true if you blow them all out with one breath."

He thought a moment then took a deep breath and blew hard. All the flames were gone. We applauded his performance. "Could you have done that with the *right* number of candles, James?" Miss Engles asked.

"That, my dear Miss Engles, is an unfair question. I shall not answer it."

While he cut the cake and served us, Miss Engles poured the tea. There was much laughter and talk of many things—books we loved, far-away places Mr. Evans had visited and Miss Engles and I hoped we might see some day. Here, suddenly, there was no room for jealousy or resentment. Only for happiness.

Later, as I rode out through the gate I looked back. They were standing together on the porch waving goodbye. Only then the whole significance of this day struck me. My heart told me I had lost my beloved! My mind told me he had never loved me as a woman, as he now loved Miss Engles. Only as a child. I wanted to cry out, to deny and accuse. The two friends I had loved most had betrayed me! Inside me was pain I'd never felt before. A frantic desire to change things, make everything right again. I knew this was impossible.

"Oh, how could you! How could you!" I sobbed aloud.

At the sound Midnight stopped and turned her head. I patted her neck. "*You* understand, don't you? Now you're my only love."

I could not go home, not yet. I couldn't face Mama or anyone while my heart was breaking. They would know something was wrong and ask questions I couldn't answer. I picked up the reins and turned Midnight off the narrow prairie path. There was a place, a deep buffalo-wallow filled with soft grass, where I could be alone. I had discovered it one spring day when the cows wandered to the far edge of our pasture which bordered the Simpson farm. Tired from my long walk that day I had rested in the cool green wallow. Thereafter it was *my place*—a place for daydreams and secret thoughts. I told no one about it. It was there I had gone to read the first book of poems Mr. Evans had lent me, *Sonnets from the Portuguese*. Now I needed its quiet secret seclusion.

I urged Midnight to a gallop, carefully avoiding the adjoining cornfield where I knew Papa was working. Tears came into my eyes, quickly dried by the wind in my face. Cattle grazed in small contented groups. They lifted their heads as I rode past then returned to leisurely munching. Soon there was only prairie emptiness. A little farther on was *my place*.

Suddenly Midnight stumbled. The reins were jerked from my hands. I pitched forward over her head, landing hard. Fiery pain shot through my leg. Dazed, I tried to get up but fell back, weak and sick with pain. The prairie turned upside down and whirled crazily. I lay very still hoping it would stop. I could hear Midnight moving about. Thank goodness, she hadn't run away! Gradually my head cleared. I knew now my leg was broken. Even if I could get to Midnight I would never be able to mount. Beyond, not more than twenty feet away, was the buffalo-wallow I'd been trying to reach. So near, yet too far! I couldn't even crawl to it. Each time I tried a great wave of blackness swallowed me. At last I gave up. What good would it do to reach it now anyway? No one would look for me there.

The afternoon sun was hot. I wondered how long it would be before someone at home missed me. It would be a couple of hours before Mama got back from town and realized I hadn't returned from my errand. The cornfield where Papa was working was too far for him to hear even if I screamed as loud as I could. If only there was some way I could get Midnight to go home without me! Vina would know something was wrong and get help. But Midnight would never leave me. She would wait patiently as she always did when I came to this place.

I looked at the sky. The sun was moving too fast toward the end of day. Overwhelmed by fear and despair I buried my face in the grass and wept. The tears were for all that had happened today, for the hopelessness I now felt. How could anything ever be right again!

At first I thought the sound was an echo of my sobbing. Then it came again, "Hello, there!"

I tried to rise, to call out, but the effort brought the blackness again. Gradually I became aware of another sound, the soft padding of horses hooves on prairie grass. And then someone was bending over me.

"Ann! Ann!" Through a hazy mist I saw it was Tom Simpson.

"Oh, Tom! Tom! I'm so glad . . . ."

He tried to lift me up but the pain in my leg made me scream. "I think it's broken. I can't move."

He knelt beside me and wiped my tears and straightened my skirt. I hadn't noticed before it was above my knees, caught under me.

"Easy, now. I'll make you comfortable as I can then go for help. I won't be gone long. You'll be all right. Just don't try to move."

Gently he pulled the folds of my skirt from under me and smoothed it over my legs. Every little movement brought a stab of pain. I gritted my teeth to keep from crying out.

Neither of us heard or saw Papa until he stood over us.

"What the devil's going on here?" he shouted. Without waiting for an answer he grabbed Tom by the hair and jerked him to his feet, and struck him hard across the face with the back of his hand. The blow sent Tom reeling.

I screamed. "Don't, Papa! Don't! Midnight . . . ."

"I'll deal with you later!" he yelled and started toward Tom.

Tom was on his feet again now. "Listen, Mr. Bullard! You don't understand. Ann's horse . . . ."

"I understand enough, you young whelp! I ought to take a bull-whip to you!" Papa lunged at Tom again. I watched, too terrifed to scream.

But Tom was on guard this time. He struck hard. Papa staggered back. "Now *listen* to me, Mr. Bullard! I don't want to fight you. Ann's hurt. Her horse threw her. I think her leg is broken."

Papa stared at both of us. His eyes were still blazing with anger.

"It's true, Papa! Tom was only trying to help me."

He was speechless only for a second. "What were you doing here in the first place?"

I told him I was on my way home. Midnight had stumbled and thrown me. Tom had found me and was going to get help. He didn't believe me.

"You came here to meet him, didn't you? You've been meeting him behind my back!"

"No, Papa. Honest! I was just riding. Tom found me, that's all."

"If you're lying to me, Ann, I'll whale the daylights out of you. Right now I've got to get you home and fetch Dr. Matthews. The springwagon's down at the end of the cornfield." He faced Tom. "I'll deal with you later, young man! Go unsaddle Midnight and bring me the blanket."

He spread the blanket on the grass and lifted me gently on-

59

to it. Tom took the corners at one end, Papa at the other, making a hammock. We started toward the cornfield. I must have lost consciousness. The next thing I knew I was in my own bed and Mama was sitting beside me.

"Oh, Mama, Mama . . . !"

"Now, now, child! Just lie still and rest. You're going to be all right. Dr. Matthews just left." Her hand on my forehead was so comforting I began to cry. She held me in her arms a while and let me cry. Then gently put me down. "Sometimes tears are the best medicine," she said.

Vina and Lucy and Mae came to the doorway. Mama told them my leg was broken. "Dr. Matthews set it and left some medicine to make her sleep. When she wakes up you can come in and visit." They went away quietly.

"Where's Papa? Oh, Mama, he wouldn't believe me . . . ."

"We'll talk about that when you wake up. Papa's very worried about you. Go to sleep now, like a good girl. Broken bones heal quickly. I'll be here if you need me." She turned the lamp down low and left the door ajar.

I tried to think of all that had happened but my mind felt fuzzy, like cotton, and my thoughts got tangled up in it. Pretty soon I was drifting somewhere in a thick grey fog. I didn't try to think any more.

The room was filled with sunlight when I awakened. There was a bunch of buttercups and snapdragons on the table by my bed. The house was quiet. I tried to sit up but one leg was so heavy I could scarcely move it. Then I remembered everything, and lay back down. Mama must have heard me stirring. She came in with a glass of milk and a bowl of oatmeal on a tray.

"Well, you look bright and shining this morning! How do you feel? I hope you're hungry."

I told her I felt fine. And my body did except for the clumsy leg. My mind was filled with dark thoughts about yesterday. I wondered what medicine Dr. Matthews might have to heal a broken heart.

"The flowers are very pretty, Mama."

"The girls picked them early this morning. You were still asleep."

"Where are they?" I really wanted to know where Papa was but was afraid to ask.

"Vina and Lucy took the cows to pasture. Mae is watering the garden. They'll be in pretty soon to get ready for Sunday school. Papa will take them."

"Aren't you going to church? I'll be all right, Mama."

"I'm sure you will, honey. But I'd rather not leave you alone. Eat your breakfast, now. You can't hurry the knitting of broken bones, but good food will help. As soon as I get the girls off to church I'll bring you something to read."

I didn't want anything to read but I didn't tell her that. Books would only remind me of Mr. Evans and that our wonderful times together were gone forever.

Vina came in and we talked while she dressed for Sunday School. Lucy and Mae came in a little later to see how I was. "You're lucky," Lucy said. "No work to do. Just lie there and read all day."

"Would you like to change places with me, smarty?"

"Well . . . no. I guess I wouldn't want my leg broken. Does it hurt a lot?"

"Not now. It just feels funny, and heavy."

When they left I waited for Papa. I heard him come out of his room, then his footsteps going down stairs. He hadn't even said good morning!

After they had left for church, Mama came back upstairs. She said Tom Simpson had stopped by to see how I was. I knew why he hadn't come in. Poor Tom! He had only wanted to help and got a beating for his trouble.

Mama had dinner ready when they got back from church. Vina came up to change her dress and told me how sorry everyone was about my accident. "Rev. Pritchard sent best wishes and said he'd come by to see you during the week." There was no message from Mr. Evans or Miss Engles.

After dinner Papa came to my room alone. He didn't ask how I was and he didn't smile. He pulled a chair close to the bed and sat down and looked at me a while before he said anything.

"Doc Matthews says you'll be all right, just a broken bone and nothing to worry about." When I didn't say anything he went on. "Now, young lady, I want to know what you and

Tom were doing way off there by yourselves, and I want the truth. Did you go there to meet him? Had you met him there before?"

"No, Papa. I told you the truth when you found us. I *was* just riding. Tom happened to come by after Midnight stumbled and threw me. I never went anywhere to meet Tom alone. Honest, Papa! Why don't you believe me?"

I tried to keep the tears back but couldn't.

"No sense bawling about it. I don't believe you because I know you're hiding something. The sooner you tell me what it is, the better. Make no mistake, Ann, I intend to get the truth one way or another."

Suddenly I was afraid. Of course I was hiding something, but not what Papa thought. What if he found out about the times I had been alone with Mr. Evans? Would he make it seem mean and ugly? Maybe fight him the way he had Tom? Or forbid me ever to go again? These thoughts were horrifying. I turned my back to Papa and buried my head in my pillow, and cried so hard Mama came to see what was wrong.

"Can't you leave her alone, Sam?" she said sharply. "She's had a terrible shock."

"She'll get more than that if she doesn't stop lying to me. She's been sneaking out to meet that Simpson boy the way Elsie did with Jed. I won't have it, Molly! I'll whale the daylights out of them both if I have to."

"You will not whale anyone, Sam. Now get out of here and let Ann rest before I lose *my* temper."

Papa went, mumbling to himself. Mama sat down on the bed and dried my tears. "It's all right, honey. Papa's just angry with himself. When he cools off he'll see things differently. Go to sleep now. You'll feel a lot better in the morning." She pulled the shades and went downstairs. I lay there thinking about what Papa said. How could I make him believe me? I could hear them talking in the kitchen below. After a while the screen door slammed and everything was quiet.

If I had known then the terrible decision Papa had reached I would not have slept at all.

# CHAPTER VI
## 1895

The week passed slowly. Uncle Ethan and Aunt Hilda drove over on Monday about the time Mama had her washing on the line. This meant they had either let their work wait to come to see me, or had gotten up earlier than usual. She brought me some ginger cookies with little candies on top. The kind she knew I liked so much. Uncle Ethan teased me a little about falling off my horse. He knew Midnight had stumbled but he pretended I didn't know how to ride. I couldn't help but feel better with them around.

The next day Elsie and little Davey came. Mrs. Phillips sent word with Vina that we would continue the music lessons at our house as soon as I was able to be downstairs. Still Papa stayed away. I knew he believed I was a bad girl, but he didn't say so again after Mama's scolding. I wondered why I had heard nothing from Mr. Evans and Miss Engles. They *must* know about my accident. Didn't they care at all? Several times that week when my unhappiness seemed too great to endure alone, I tried to tell Mama why I had ridden off by myself that day. Each time the words stuck in my throat. I *couldn't* let her know how foolish I had been. I'd had time to think about it and now knew that it was foolish to fall in love with a man so much older than I was, who didn't love me at all. He loved Miss Engles. Sometimes when I was alone I wept for my lost dream.

Dr. Matthews came by the middle of the week. I'd never seen him on any of our trips to town and was unconscious when he set my leg. I liked him at once. He was a roly-poly little man with thinning hair, and there was gentleness in his eyes magnified by thick-lensed glasses. He examined my leg, took my temperature and checked my pulse. "You're doing fine, young lady. A broken bone is nothing to worry about, just part of growing up." He put the instrument back in his bag and sat down beside the bed. "What *I* should be worrying about is a rash of broken hearts in these parts. You're a mighty pretty young lady, Miss Bullard." He winked at me. "Even an old man like myself can see that."

He followed Mama downstairs to the kitchen. I could hear them talking. "Her leg is all right but I don't understand why her temperature stays up. It should be normal by this time. She has no internal injuries. If she weren't a child I'd say she has something on her mind—something she is keeping bottled up inside her. Do you know of anything to cause this?"

I thought Mama might tell him about Papa's accusations, but she didn't. "She's had a shock, that's all. It can be a very frightening thing to find yourself alone on the prairie with night coming on, unable to move. We must give her time. She'll be all right I'm sure." I heard the back screen door open. "Thank you for coming, Doctor. And please tell Donald I may be a little late getting in on Saturday but I'll be there."

Mama came back upstairs. "Is there anything you want, dear?" I shook my head. "Perhaps something I can bring from town on Saturday? A new book, or a magazine? I know how tiresome it must be just lying there all day. But Dr. Matthews says you should be up and about very soon."

I told her I didn't feel like reading, but she wasn't to worry about me. I'd just rest and think. After a minute or two she pulled a chair to the bedside. "Do you want to talk about it, darling?"

My bravery melted. Tears filled my eyes. "It *was* an accident, Mama! Papa won't believe me. He thinks I'm a bad girl. I'm not, Mama. Honest I'm not! Why won't he believe me? You believe me, don't you?"

She smoothed my hair from my forehead and kissed me. "Of course you're not a bad girl! Papa doesn't believe that either. He's just upset. Now dry those tears and let me fix your pillows. Then I'll bring you a nice cold glass of buttermilk."

I would have told her then about Mr. Evans and Miss Engles, that it wasn't only Papa I was grieving about, if Mae hadn't come bursting in with a big bunch of daisies for me. By the time they were in a vase beside my bed and Mae had gone back downstairs, the moment for confession had passed. I couldn't think of a way to begin, or find the courage for it.

Mama made doughnuts the next morning. The spicy, tantalizing aroma drifted up to me through the register and the stairway. I heard a knock on the kitchen door. It was Rev. Pritchard. "I was driving past and caught that delightful cooking aroma," he said cheerily.

Mama said, "Come right in, sir! They're just about ready to fish out of the frying fat." It was good to hear her so light-hearted.

"The truth is, I came by to see how Ann is, and bring her some magazines. How is she?"

"Why don't you go on upstairs and ask her yourself? I'll bring a plate of doughnuts and lemonade in a minute. She will enjoy some company."

I sat up and smoothed my hair and tried to see myself in the mirror above the dresser. It stood catty-cornered so I got only a glimpse of part of me. I just hoped I looked all right, and that my secret didn't show. I liked Rev. Pritchard and was glad he had come to see me. He was kind and gentle and pleasant, not stuffy and solemn as other preachers I had met. At community dances he was always smiling. He seemed to enjoy watching others having a good time although he never joined the dancing. I wondered why. Probably because most folks would think it sinful for a preacher to enjoy himself. He could be serious, though, when there were problems, and he had a comforting way with sick people. Still no one could say he didn't enjoy the life he had chosen—serving the Lord.

"Good morning, Ann." He came to the bedside and looked down at me, smiling. "For an invalid I must say you look quite fit, young lady."

I returned his smile and ask him to sit down. He brought a chair from across the room and sat down beside the little table with the vase of daisies. "Mae brought them yesterday. Aren't they pretty?" What *did* one say to a minister when he came calling?

"Indeed they are. We've missed you at church." He didn't say he was sorry about the accident, and that pleased me. I'd heard that so many times. He said, "Broken bones, fortunately, heal quickly. But they can be quite a nuisance in the process. Still, you can go to the Fourth of July picnic, can't you?"

"I don't think so. Dr. Matthews says I have to be quiet."

He smiled. "I'm not suggesting you join in the square dancing."

We laughed about that, the idea of a one-legged square dancer. "I understand there's going to be a big fireworks display, and there is sure to be plenty of ice cream and cake and lemonade," he went on. "No reason you can't enjoy them."

No reason, I thought, except that Papa would never permit me to go. He wouldn't let me go anywhere or even speak to me unless I admitted I had been lying. When I glanced up, Rev. Pritchard was looking at me rather strangely.

Mama came in with lemonade and a plate of doughnuts. She visited a while then left us alone. I wished she hadn't. I was beginning to get an awful feeling that he knew my secret. Was it possible for a minister to know things by instinct that others couldn't know? I relaxed a little when he began telling me amusing incidents that had happened to him when he was a boy growing up in Philadelphia.

"There was one boy, Billy Martin, who used to wait behind a fence for us kids when we came out of church on Sunday all dressed in our best clothes. All he wanted to do was fight. We kept out of his way if we could while we had on our good clothes, but there were plenty of black eyes in the neighborhood that year. We older boys could take care of ourselves but when he started picking on the little kids we knew something had to be done."

He paused to finish a second doughnut and comment on how good they were. "What did you do?" I asked, really wanting to know.

"We laid a trap for him, but Billy was smart. He waited for us on the other side of the street the next Sunday and pelted us with ripe tomatoes. Our clothes were a sorry sight, and so were we. We could wash our faces in the watering trough but there was nothing we could do about our clothes. We knew—and Billy knew—we would get a tanning from our fathers for fighting on Sunday."

"But you didn't start the fight. Couldn't you tell your papas that?"

"We could but they wouldn't believe us. Papa always said it took two to make a fight, and we must have done something to the other boy to make him start the fight. So I didn't try to tell him what had happened. I took my punishment. It didn't seem fair, though, to be punished for something I didn't do."

The way Papa was punishing me! My heart almost stopped beating. He *did* know my secret! He wouldn't have told me that story if he didn't. But how? Did Papa talk to him, or Mama?

"I think I understand, Rev. Pritchard," I said, hoping he would change the subject. He didn't.

"My friend, Joey, and I decided Billy had to be taught a lesson some way. One Sunday when we had made sure he was waiting behind the fence for us with a bucket of tomatoes, we slipped out the back door of the church and circled the block so we could come up behind him. Before he knew what was happening Joey had one arm and I the other. We dunked him in the horse trough until he begged for mercy."

"I'll bet *he* got the tanning that day," I laughed, dismissing my suspicions. Rev. Pritchard was just trying to cheer me up.

"I don't know about that. But he did stop picking on the little kids. I don't think I wanted him to get punished, even if he did deserve it. I felt rather sorry for him. He didn't have much else to do *but* fight. It was a long time before I understood that he was only trying to even things up a little. We had good clothes and nice homes, he didn't. He had to prove he was a better fighter than we were."

"I don't see . . ."

"How that evened things up? It didn't, really. It just made Billy think they were so he could endure what he had to. His parents never went to church and they wouldn't let Billy go. Billy used to say over and over, 'Sissies! Sissies! Only sissies go to Sunday school,' and start throwing his ripe tomatoes."

"Did you always want to be a minister? I mean, did you know then what you wanted to do when you grew up?"

"In a way I suppose I did, Ann. I never liked violence of any kind. It seemed so senseless. It never settled anything, just made them worse. Even while we were teaching Billy 'a lesson' as we thought we were doing, I kept wishing it didn't have to be done that way. Why couldn't we just make friends with him instead?"

"Did you try to do that?"

"Not hard enough, I guess. But I went around trying to make peace between kids who were fighting until they began to gang up on me. You see, Ann, they didn't want peace. Fighting seemed to make them feel they were men. So I let them alone, and started looking out for stray dogs and cats."

"I'm sure they appreciated that. The cats and dogs, I mean."

He laughed. "They did, but my father didn't. Mother let me feed the strays under the back porch, but I lived in daily fear my father would discover them and make me drown every one of them."

"Would he really do that?"

"Oh, yes, indeed! Not because he didn't like animals. He did. But not in such numbers. A cat or a dog had its uses, he'd say. Too many of them would 'eat you out of the house and home', if you didn't get rid of them fast."

"What did you do?"

"Nothing for a while. But it bothered me that, in a way, I was lying to my father, not telling him about the strays. Keeping something from him was *almost* the same as lying, I told myself. And then I would remember the verse on our Sunday school cards that said, 'Suffer the little children to come unto me . . .' Cats and dogs weren't people, of course, but they *were* God's creatures, weren't they? And the Bible said God loved all His creatures great and small. It was very puzzling."

"Why didn't you ask your mother what to do about it?"

"Oh, that wouldn't have been fair. You see *I* had created the problem, if it was a problem. It was up to me to find the solution. And I knew what I had to do. Find homes for all those strays." He laughed. "I must have walked a hundred miles and knocked on as many doors before I accomplished that."

He was silent a moment. "And do you know what pleased me the most? Not only that I had found homes for my strays, but that I had been able to do it without hurting my father. I understood, then, that I hadn't been lying to him, only trying to do what I felt was right without hurting him. I think that is when I knew, Ann, that I wanted to spend my life helping the helpless. Helping them God's way. I was fourteen now and somehow I knew that was what God wanted me to do, too."

Listening to him I'd completely forgotten my problem, but I was sure he had told me that story for a purpose. Maybe his father was much like Papa, someone you couldn't reason with. And for the first time I saw Rev. Pritchard as a person, not just "our preacher". I'd thought ministers weren't like other people, that they were just naturally good and kind without sins or temptations; that in some miraculous way *they* had never had to be kids who got into mischief and had to be punished, or had trouble deciding what they wanted to be when they grew up.

He took out his watch. "My goodness! I had no idea I'd been talking so long. Forgive me, Ann! But you *are* very easy to talk to, you know."

"I enjoyed listening, Rev. Pritchard. Truly I did. and I feel a lot better. Thank you for coming, and for the magazines."

Mama came upstairs. She glanced at the empty doughnut plate. "Shall I bring more?"

He said quickly, "Oh, no, please. They were delicious but I've already eaten too many."

"Well, you'd *better* like them," Mama teased. "I've made an extra dozen for you to take home with you." She glanced at me. "Your visit certainly has done Ann a lot of good. Thank you for taking time to visit with her."

"My pleasure, I assure you. And I'm going to expect to see her at the Fourth of July picnic. I may just come and get her myself, with your permission, Mrs. Bullard."

"We'll see how she feels by that time."

Long after he had gone I thought about the things he had said. It was comforting to feel that if he did know my secret, he would understand. If only Papa would! Each night when he came home from the fields I'd wait hopefully, listening for his steps on the stairs. But he never came. Not until after supper when he came up to bed, and even then he never came into my room. It was Mama or Vina who brought me my supper, and Mama who came to kiss me good-night. Tom did not come to see me again. Or if he did stop by I was not told about it. Maybe he stayed away because Papa had ordered him to. Had Papa also ordered Mr. Evans to stay away? He must know something had happened to me when I didn't take the butter and eggs as usual.

Then suddenly I forgot about Mr. Evans.

One evening, about a week after my accident, I was listening to the family conversation drifting up to me through the floor-register and wondering why Mama had not brought my supper before they started eating, as she usually did. Presently there was a sharp sound like a slap, and Papa's voice, loud and angry.

"Don't lie to me! I know what I saw! Next time I'll take a buggy whip to both of you!"

Mama's voice, shocked. "Sam!"

Vina came running up the stairs and burst into the room. She threw herself onto the bed sobbing, "I hate him! I hate him!"

The angry voices went on below. I couldn't hear what they were saying because of Vina's crying. "Please don't cry, honey. Tell me what happened." She only cried harder. I let her cry. After a while she stopped and turned over on her back, staring up at the ceiling.

"He slapped me! I wasn't lying. Honest, I wasn't Ann!"

"About what? Why did he slap you?"

"Because he's mean and I hate him! I'll hate him the rest of my life!"

I heard the screen door slam. There was stillness below and here in my room. Vina got up and paced about but she still hadn't told me what had happened. After a while Mama came upstairs. She told Vina to sit down, pacing wasn't going to help anything, and put her arm around her. Vina cried a while before she told us what Papa was mad about.

She had been bringing the cows home from pasture when she saw Gus Gruder riding toward her. She stopped and waited for him. Some of his cattle had strayed and he thought they might have gotten in with ours. When he found they hadn't he had ridden along with her intending to cut across the pasture to the Simpson farm. That was when Papa came out of the corn-field and saw them.

"He thinks I was with Gus all afternoon, Mama. I told him I wasn't, but he won't believe me."

All my hatred for him boiled up inside me. Wasn't it enough

70

he was treating me the way he was? Did he have to treat Vina the same way? What was wrong with him, anyway?

Mama comforted her. "I'll make him understand, honey. Dry your tears now and get ready for bed. You'll feel better in the morning."

But nothing was better the next morning. Everything was much worse. Papa stormed and shouted and ordered everyone around the way he used to do, even Mama. He made Vina go to the fields with him every morning after chores and work all day. Mama protested and tried to reason with him. It did no good. I knew that when I could walk again the same fate awaited me.

"What's happened to Papa? Why is he doing this to you?" I asked Vina after a week of it.

"Nothing's happened to him. He's just mean, that's all. He says we've had things too easy. Says Mama's spoiled us with her money and fancy ideas. All we need, he says, is some hard work to bring us to our senses. Oh, Ann, he goes on like that for hours! What are we going to do?"

We both knew there was nothing we could do. If Mama couldn't reason with Papa, what chance did we have? Waiting for Papa to explode with temper, once more became a part of our lives. We dreaded the days Mama had to go to town.

One Saturday, a couple of weeks after my accident, Mama had gone to town as usual telling Lucy to stay close to the house in case I needed anything. I was lying there thinking of all our problems, and wondering why Mr. Evans had not at least sent me a message. He could have done that no matter how busy he might be, couldn't he? Maybe I'd just be an invalid the rest of my life, like Elizabeth Barrett Browning. And write poetry. *That* would tell him how much I had loved him! And Papa would have to believe me and be kind.

Then I heard Mr. Evans' voice in the kitchen below.

"Good morning, Lucy. How is Ann today?"

My heart leaped with joy. He had come! He *did* care! And then I remembered this was the day he got his supply of butter and eggs. He hadn't come to see me at all! But why hadn't Mama taken them to him on her way to town? And why hadn't he come before if he cared?

I could hear him talking with Lucy in the kitchen. After a

while he came upstairs. He sat down beside the bed and took both my hands. "I'm deeply distressed by all this, my dear. I've only just learned about what happened from Ethan. I've been away—in Sioux City. But *how* did it happen?"

So he *hadn't* stayed away on purpose! I told him about Midnight stumbling and throwing me. "My leg is broken, but Dr. Matthews says it will heal quickly."

"Dr. Matthews is right. Broken bones seem to be a painful part of youth. Nature's way of reminding us we aren't indestructible."

"He says something like that, too. But I don't think I needed this reminder."

He stayed a while, visiting with me until Lucy had counted the eggs and wrapped the butter. She came up to tell him they were ready.

"I can't stay to have tea with you today, my dear. But I shall come back next week. Perhaps your mother can find time to bake some of those delicious sugar cookies for us."

"I'm sure she will."

At the door he turned. "One good thing about broken bones, they keep you in bed for a while with plenty of time for reading. When I come again I'll bring you a book or two."

It was almost dark when Mama got home. Vina and Lucy had been working in the garden all afternoon, with Mae trailing after them. Now they were cooling off under the cottonwood in the back yard. It had been a very hot day. Mama came upstairs as soon as the supplies were put away, and I told her about Mr. Evans' visit.

"Did you know he has been away, Mama?"

"Yes. Uncle Ethan told me he was checking on some stock he might want to buy. I didn't know he was back or I'd have taken the produce to him this morning."

"Why doesn't Miss Engles come to see me?"

"How can she, honey? Didn't you know she went back east for the summer? She left right after school was out."

"No, I didn't know, Mama." But the world was suddenly brighter.

Mama went back downstairs to start supper. I saw Papa come in from the barn and stop to say something to Vina. She went to the barn, and the others followed him inside. Pretty

72

soon Vina came in and all the girls came upstairs to change their clothes. I could hear the creak of the kitchen pump, and Papa say something to Mama, but I couldn't hear what he said with the water running.

Suddenly Mama's voice rose sharply "Sam! You *didn't!* You couldn't be so cruel!"

"Call it cruel if you want to. I did what I had to do. You've spoiled these kids rotten ever since you got that money from your pa. It's time they had some discipline."

"But surely, Sam . . ."

"I don't want to hear any more about it. If those kids had been working in the fields with me they wouldn't have gone galivantin' off on the prairie with any boy that asked 'em."

"Stop it, Sam Bullard! You know very well what happened in both instances but you're too stubborn to admit *you* are wrong. No, you'd rather take it out on the girls. Well, I won't have it! You can't do . . ."

"Stop telling me what I can't do. It's done. I'll show those kids who's boss around here even if you *are* too big for your britches."

Mama held her temper. I knew it wasn't because she was afraid of him; she hadn't been afraid of Papa for a long time. She probably didn't want to upset us girls.

Vina looked at me. "What in the world has Papa done now?"

"It must be something pretty awful for Mama to shout at him."

"Maybe I can find out." She went downstairs. When she came back she had my supper-tray, but she hadn't learned anything more.

I ate very little of my supper, listening to what was happening downstairs. No one said very much except to ask someone to pass something. Then the screen door slammed and I knew Papa had gone out. Mama told Lucy and Mae to go feed the chickens. She and Vina came upstairs.

"What's wrong, Mama?"

She sat down on the side of my bed and pulled Vina down beside her. "I don't know any easy way to tell you girls what I must. Papa has sold Midnight and Golden."

# CHAPTER VII
## 1895

Papa left the house right after breakfast Sunday morning. Vina had refused to go downstairs until he left.

"I'll never speak to him again as long as I live!" she vowed.

"That won't change anything. But it *will* hurt Mama. Is that what you want?"

"Of course not!"

"Then let's use our heads. I've been thinking. Papa will expect us to sulk over what he did. He *wants* us to complain. If we don't he'll think we don't care. Then *he'll* feel sorry, or be a lot madder because we're not being 'disciplined' the way he planned."

"But that won't get our horses back."

"No. I think it will make Mama happier, though."

Vina finally agreed. We would ignore what Papa had done, not even mention it. For Vina it was a kind of play-acting. For me, stubbornness. I refused to give Papa the satisfaction of knowing how much he had hurt me. Selling Midnight on top of everything else he had done to punish me. Both of us could keep silent about the whole thing but neither of us could stop thinking about it. Vina's pretended cheerfulness made my heart ache. Inside I knew she wanted to cry her eyes out. And she would have if it would have brought Golden back.

I had plenty of time to think. This, and the change in Papa, were all my fault. Mama seldom smiled now. When she did I was sure it was only to make me feel better. Papa ate his meals but said little to anyone. The only bright note in my days was anticipation of Mr. Evans' promised visit. I counted the days until Saturday. Mama baked sugar cookies on Friday.

"If he doesn't come early I can't wait for him," she told me Saturday morning. "But I'll leave the butter and eggs in the cellar where they'll keep cool. Looks like it's going to be a hot day. Lucy'll stay close by and watch for him."

It was after ten o'clock when he came. Mama had been gone

for more than an hour. Lucy brought him upstairs and left us alone. She would prepare tea and bring it up in half an hour, as I'd asked her to do.

He hadn't brought the books he'd promised. I wondered why. Had he forgotten them? He inquired about how I felt and again assured me broken bones healed quickly when one was young. Then he chuckled to himself.

"I was remembering *my* first broken bone," he said. "I was twelve. I tried to climb an apple tree I'd been forbidden to climb. *This* Humpty Dumpty had a great fall, indeed. And a broken leg."

"Why did you climb it if you were told not to?"

"Boys that age often do what they are told not to do. They always have a good reason, at least satisfactory to themselves, for disobedience. With me it was simply that I *had* to get two big red apples from the top of the tree. For Susan. Ah, she was the prettiest girl in the world. I was quite convinced of that. She had promised to be my girl and let we walk home from school with her every afternoon if I'd get those apples for her."

"Was that the only apple tree?"

"Oh, no. And there were plenty of apples on the lower branches. But Susan always wanted what was out of reach, and I had to prove how much I liked her." He smiled. "You see Harry liked her too and he wasn't afraid of anything. Disobeying my parents seemed a small price to pay for her favors."

I laughed. "And you got a broken leg for your trouble."

"Yes, but the lesson I learned was worth it. Dear, selfish little Susan! By the time I could walk again she had forgotten all about my derring-do. Harry was walking her home after school."

"I don't see why you call her 'dear Susan.' I think she was awful. Did she marry Harry?"

"Oh, no. Not little Susan! That autum a new boy caught her fancy. He had his own carriage and a beautiful chestnut mare. Susan didn't walk home from school that season." He sighed and smiled. "Would you believe it, Ann, it took me a whole semester to recover from my broken heart. That spring I noticed the girl next door had grown up. She was a lot prettier than Susan."

I laughed with him over the story, but I wondered if he had told it to me for a purpose, as I suspected Rev. Pritchard had done. Did he suspect, or know, why I had ridden off alone that day?

To change the subject I asked, "Did you forget to bring me a book?"

"Forgive me. I seem to have got carried away with my own story." He took a small book from his coat pocket and handed it to me.

I studied the title. *The Rubaiyat of Omar Khayyam.* I stumbled over the pronunciation and we laughed about that. He spoke the words slowly and I repeated them after him.

"Such a strange name," I mused.

"Omar was a Persian poet-astronomer." He went on to tell me about the man who had lived hundreds of years ago, and of Saki, the girl he loved.

Lucy brought the tea tray on schedule and departed. This, I thought, was almost as nice as having tea in his library. At least he was here!

He picked up the story again. "Khayyam. It isn't an easy name, is it? Nor was his life during those turbulent and cruel years when Persian history was being forced into new paths. But, as frequently happens, much good came from all that strife and terror. Omar spent his life studying and teaching new sciences. For many years he was ridiculed by the so-called wise men of his time. But in time, legend tells us, Omar Khayyam became the wisest of all. He was unrivaled in science, especially astronomy. Because of his wide-spread teachings men began to put away their superstitions about the heavens and to understand something of the universe."

Listening to him was suddenly like being carried to that far-away land. How insignificant, I thought, were the things that troubled me! Always he made me see the bigness of life and places and people. Surely he was the wisest man I'd ever know.

Suddenly a terrible thought struck me. What if Papa came to the house before Mr. Evans left? What would he say and do?

Mr. Evans misinterpreted my anxiety which must have shown in my face. He got up and set the teacup on the tray. "I've tried you with all my talk, Ann. Forgive me. I'll be on my way now. And you get well soon. I miss our little visits."

I didn't want him to go but I knew it was best he did. I

thanked him for coming and especially for the book. "I know I shall enjoy it very much."

"Just so long as you don't take Omar's philosophy too seriously! He was a poet, you must remember, with his own ideas about life and the hereafter. It has only now occurred to me that Rev. Pritchard might not approve of your reading the book at all. Or your parents. But we won't make a secret of it."

I thought about that after he had gone. Was there special meaning in his last remark? As for approval, certainly Papa would not approve — either of the book or Mr. Evans lending it to me. Mama might consider it "over my head" but she agreed with Mr. Evans that books should stretch one's mind. Until a few days ago I would have been sure Rev. Pritchard would instantly disapprove. Now I understood him better. He didn't believe a person had to be "against" everything in order to do God's work.

It was the end of June before I was able to be moved downstairs. Mama made a pallet on the parlor sofa for me. When she went to town on Saturday she brought back a pair of crutches. As soon as Papa was out of the house each morning I practiced walking with them. It was a clumsy, slow process.

What was I in such a hurry about, anyway, I asked myself? Papa would put me to work as soon as I could so much as crawl. The burden of my own guilt weighed heavily upon me. I *had* to do something to make things right again. But what could I do? In desperation I considered telling Papa the whole truth, that it was Mr. Evans I loved, not Tom. But I knew that would only make matters worse. Even if I told Mama now it would not change anything. Papa wouldn't believe her either.

Suddenly I remembered my talk with Rev. Pritchard. Surely I could tell him anything without fear or shame. He would understand and he could talk to Papa. Papa would have to believe *him!* But how could I talk to Rev. Pritchard alone? When he came to see me Mama usually visited with us too. If there was just some place . . . The picnic! He had said maybe he'd come and get me. Papa couldn't object to my going with *him*. And I'd have a chance to tell him everything and ask him to make Papa understand. It was a perfect plan. *If* I were walking well enough by then. I intended to make sure I was.

Since being moved downstairs I had supper with the rest of the family. Papa still ignored me, but Vina kept things lively. Her play-acting had now reached the "grand performance" stage, and she was the star. You'd never believe she had been working like a field-hand all day.

"Do you *have* to talk all the time, Vina?" Papa snapped a couple of times. "A man likes a little peace after a hard day's work."

"Someone should say something," Mama countered, "unless mealtime is to seem more like a funeral."

Tonight Papa seemed in a little better humor. I got up the courage to mention the picnic. "Rev. Pritchard wants to take me and I'm well enough now."

"If you're well enough for picnics you're well enough to help with the work." He looked across the table at Mama. "Ben told me today the harvesters will be here first thing Monday morning."

"The picnic's on Saturday, Sam. We can all go and still be ready for work on Monday."

"No we can't. We're not going. That's final." He finished his coffee and went outside. He could always escape when things became unpleasant, we couldn't. Or even have the last word!

"Our master's voice!" Vina announced solemnly.

"Never mind that, young lady." Mama went to the pantry and came back with a big bowl of ice cream. "I made this this afternoon. Papa didn't wait for it so you girls may have seconds tonight."

None of us went to the picnic.

The harvesting crew moved in on Monday as promised. Soon we were all too busy to think about disappointments or heartbreaks, only work. Mama and Vina cooked and baked, and carried morning and afternoon snacks to the men in the field. Lucy and Mae and I did most of the houseworrk. I could get around pretty well with my crutches, and I could sit on a high stool at the kitchen sink and peel potatoes and apples until my fingers were blistered, and wash piles of dishes every day. Lucy and Mae dried and put them away.

One afternoon when the dishes were finished and the flies

cleared from the house, Mama sat down for a cup of coffee before she started fixing the snack to take to the men. She looked so tired and worried I began to cry.

"It's all my fault, Mama! My fault . . . my fault!"

Mama put her arms around me and helped me down from the stool. "You're just over-tired. Come lie down for a while."

"No! No! I don't want to lie down. It *is* my fault. Papa's mean to all of you because of me."

Nevertheless she led me into the parlor where it was cooler. The windows were kept closed and the shades drawn all day during the summer. Here the light was soft. She made me lie down on the sofa and sat beside me. Suddenly the whole story came tumbling out. About my love for Mr. Evans, and why I had gone off alone that day, and Midnight's throwing me because I wasn't watching where we were going, and how Tom found me and tried to help until Papa came.

"We weren't bad, Mama. We weren't!"

She drew me into her arms and held me a while before she spoke.

"Many things are hard to understand, dear, when we are young. Love is probably the hardest to understand. I think that is because it is the greatest thing in the world. You see there are many kinds of love, darling. Each is fine and real and beautiful. There is God's love for us and our love for Him. There is the love between a man and a woman, and their love for their children. And there is the love between friends, the kind of love Mr. Evans has for you and you for him. The love of sharing beautiful things such as books and ideas and companionship, which help you to grow into a lovely young woman. One day you will find that other kind of love — the love of a woman for the man she marries."

"Do you think that is the way Miss Engles loves Mr. Evans?"

"Perhaps. Now you must rest, dear. I have to take lunch to the men. I won't be gone long. When I get back I'll make us some lemonade." She leaned to kiss me and I threw my arms about her.

"Oh, Mama, I'm so sorry for all the trouble I've caused."

"You haven't caused any trouble, honey."

"But Papa hates me. He hates all of us. All because of what he thinks I did."

"No, darling. Papa doesn't hate you or any of us. He loves us very much. Right now he's like a fractious horse with a burr under its blanket. He won't let anyone remove it so he pitches and snorts trying to get rid of it himself. Pretty soon he'll get tired of that and stand still long enough to let someone help him."

I couldn't help laughing.

"Now, that's better! Rest now, and always remember, honey, there is no problem too big to be solved with God's help."

I lay there in the shadowy coolness after she had gone, thinking. My heart was no longer heavy. The lump which had been there so long was gone and in its place was a kind of inner glow. I now understood that loving Mr. Evans the way I did was not wrong, or even something to be kept secret. Maybe that was what he had been trying to tell me, too. That friendship was something to cherish and it could last as long as we lived.

I no longer envied Miss Engles. Nor was I jealous of his attentions to her. We could both love him, in our own way. And Miss Engles and I could be friends forever too!

Mama was gone no more than an hour but in that short time I had done a good deal of growing up. I felt different. I wasn't even afraid of Papa now. I could laugh about the "burr under his blanket," and then feel sorry for him because his suffering was needless. If he'd only listen to the truth from Vina and me, there would be nothing for him to be angry about. He wouldn't have to keep trying to "discipline" us.

One sorrow remained. The loss of Midnight and Golden. Maybe, I thought, once Papa got rid of his "burr" he would buy back the horses. No horse could take the place of Midnight. Still, if Papa bought others for us it might prove he believed we hadn't misbehaved. Everything would be all right again.

However, this was only day-dreaming now. Papa still had his "burr."

The dreadful back-breaking work of wheat harvest was finally over. Golden shocks of grain stood ready for the threshers. The harvest crews moved on to other fields. Once more there was only the family for meals. Papa still remained glumly silent most of the time and left each morning for the fields. Mama and Vina milked the cows. Lucy drove them to pasture and fed and watered the horses. Mae carried small buckets of water to pour along the thirsty rows in the vegetable garden. With this task I could help. I could manage short distances quite well now without my crutches.

The following week Dr. Matthews came to remove the splints and bandages. He warned me to take things easy for a while. "No dancing, young lady!" I could have told him there wasn't much chance of that while Papa felt the way he did.

I had seen Mr. Evans briefly each week when he came for butter and eggs. Now I could think of him as a good friend and know that he was. If he had time we would talk a while about some book I had read recently, or one he had lent me. And once when he came in the afternoon, Mama served tea in the parlor.

Rev. Pritchard usually stopped by one day of the week and stayed to chat a while. Tom had made no effort to see me again, and sent no message. To myself I made all kinds of excuses for him. He was just busy with harvest like everyone else. Or he stayed away because he didn't want to make more trouble for me. I remembered the story Mr. Evans had told me about Susan. Had Tom found another girl? Surprisingly, the thought did not make me unhappy. I had always known I wasn't in love with Tom and was sure I never could be. Not the way I now knew a girl *should* feel toward the boy she wanted to marry. Besides, if Tom had really loved *me*, he would have braved Papa's anger, or anything, just to see me.

August brought the dreaded dog-days. An endless time of hot dry winds which rustled drying leaves and beat down upon barren fields swirling dust into little cyclones to deposit thick grey film over everything. Mama kept most of the windows closed throughout the house, and shades drawn. Usually she opened them at night to let in cool air. Now there was no coolness in the breeze that stirred the cottonwood leaves. The nights were sticky hot. The windmill wheel stood motionless. Dry crackling sounds and the high piping of many crickets filled the night.

It was a time of apprehension. This was cyclone weather. Much as we needed rain we watched any building up of dark, yellowish clouds with anxiety. One afternoon in late August Papa came from the barn to where Mama and I sat under the cottonwood shelling peas for canning.

"This time we're going to get something," he remarked, scanning the skies. "I hope it's rain and only that. But you'd better round up the kids and be ready for the storm-cellar."

Far to the west a huge bank of purplish-yellow clouds was boiling up like an overflowing kettle. It was frightening to watch, but even more terrible to think what might be happening to the farmers who lived there. Or what could be happening to us in a few minutes. Flashes of lightning splintered the sky from time to time. Thunder rumbled distantly.

Papa went back to the barn. Mama called to Vina and Lucy who were working close by in the garden. Despite the heat, all of us had worked most of the day, hoeing and watering and pulling weeds. I could walk now without crutches. Papa no longer permitted me to be idle.

We went inside. Mama gathered up things to take to the storm-cellar. "Go close the upstairs windows, Vina. Ann can see to the downstairs ones."

Suddenly Papa burst into the house. "Prairie fire! Somebody's in real trouble."

We ran outside. Now we could smell the smoke. Huge grey clouds of it billowed up, lighted now and then by licking flames. "They'll need help," Papa said and started toward the barn.

Uncle Ethan yelled from the road. "It's Jenkins' pasture!" He turned in at the gate and jumped down. "We've got to get firebreaks set before it gets to the corn and wheat fields." In the back of his wagon was a plow.

Papa harnessed a team. He and Uncle Ethan brought a plow from the shed and put it in the wagon. Mama called to them. "Harness another team. I can handle another plow."

"No, you stay here with the kids and watch for sparks. The wind's in the right direction to carry them this far. If that happens, put a saddle on Daisy and send one of the kids for me."

In minutes they were gone down the road toward the Jenkins place. We could see other farmers racing across the prairie toward the rising wall of smoke and flames.

"It's going to be hard to put that fire out. Everything's so dry." Mama shaded her eyes with her hand and peered toward wispy clouds of smoke that drifted across the Simpson pasture and ours. Even as we watched they grew thicker and darker. "You girls go back inside. I'm going to saddle Daisy. I don't like the looks of this."

We forgot our tiredness and the heat. Inside we watched from the kitchen window. The smoke was now so thick it darkened the afternoon sky. Mama came back and tied Daisy near the house. She stayed on the porch watching for sparks. None of us needed to be told what a few sparks could do to the oat and wheat fields where grain was shocked ready for threshers next week. Or the cornfield almost ready for harvesting. Or the house and barns.

The hours went by. We knew the fire was getting closer. We could hear the men shouting as they plowed firebreaks and set backfires. Others beat down flames with wet gunnysacks. Black smoke told us the fire was out in spots. Where the smoke was grey the flames still licked up prairie grass like a hungry animal.

"Will we burn up too, Mama?" Mae asked, clinging to her skirt. She and Lucy were crying.

"Hush, both of you! If the fire gets any closer Vina will go for Papa."

At first I thought the tiny flicker was my imagination, or fear. Then it burst into flames. The Simpson pasture was on fire! "Look, Mama!" I screamed.

Mama grabbed a scarf and handed it to Vina. "Tie this over your mouth and nose, and find Papa. But be careful! Stay on the road as far as you can and don't go too close to the flames. They can jump and be all around you before you know it." She helped Vina to mount Daisy. They went out the back gate at a gallop.

Mama brought another team from the barn and hitched them to a plow. "When Papa comes tell him I'm in the cornfield. And watch for sparks, Ann. With the fire so close everything is in danger. Lucy, you and Mae stay in the house and do what Ann tells you to do." She was gone.

I waited on the back porch, my eyes glued to the rooftops of barns and sheds. Every few minutes I circled the house checking its roof. It seemed hours before Vina and Papa came. I told him where Mama was. "You kids stay here. All of you." He yelled back, "And look out for sparks." He headed for Simpson's pasture. Pretty soon others joined him. We could hear their

shouts and see the flames. A sudden belch of black smoke meant
the fire had been beaten down or had reached a firebreak, Vina
and I took turns circling the house and keeping an eye on Lucy
and Mae. Vina looked very tired and her face was still black with
soot.

"It was awful! Just awful! I've never seen anything like it."
She told me she had had to ignore Mama's warning and ride
close to the fire to find Papa. "The smoke was too thick for me
to see anything if I didn't get close. My throat burned if I took
the scarf away even for a second. I couldn't even yell. I'd never
have found Papa if he hadn't seen me."

Gradually the flames seemed to be dying down. Smoldering
grass sent up black smoke which drifted across the prairie. The
danger to our house and barns seemed to be over. Still Mama
and Papa did not come back.

"If they don't get here pretty soon I'm going to look for them.
Maybe Mama's hurt."

Vina said, "What could you do by yourself? We'd better stay
right here like Papa said. If they weren't all right we'd have
known it by now. They aren't alone."

It seemed hours before we heard them at the gate, and ran to
meet them. Mama's face was streaked with soot and she looked
ready to drop. Papa's face was so black it was hard to recognize
him. His clothes were soaked.

"Is the fire really out?" we asked in one breath.

"I hope so," Papa said wearily. "Can you kids take care of
the teams?"

"Sure, Papa."

Later, when they had washed their faces and were having
coffee, Papa said an all-night watch had been set up to make sure
the fire didn't break out again. "We were mighty lucky. But poor
Jenkins. He lost most of his corn and his pastures are burned
black, but we did keep it from reaching his wheat field." He
leaned over and patted Vina's shoulder. "Thanks to your bravery,
honey. Riding into that furnace was mighty dangerous. Are you
all right?"

"Yes, Papa. Just tired."

Mama asked quickly, "What do you mean, Sam, 'riding into
that furnace'?"

Vina answered. "I know you told me to stay clear of the

flames, Mama, but I *had* to get close to find Papa. I couldn't see through the smoke."

"Good heavens!" Mama's face paled. "I should have gone myself."

"If you had," Papa said, "we might not have been so lucky. Getting that firebreak started when you did saved our cornfield. And if the fire had reached it, the oats and wheat would have gone too."

"We're all safe and unhurt. That's what is important," Mama said.

Papa looked like he agreed with her. All he said was, "We better get to bed."

## CHAPTER VIII
## 1895

The threshing crew came the following Monday. We were so thankful to have grain to thresh no one complained about the work. Papa and several other farmers shared corn with Mr. Jenkins. His cattle and some of ours grazed in various pastures. Except for the blackened land the prairie fire was soon just something unfortunate that had happened. A part of prairie life along with cyclones and blizzards.

September came with light rainfall. Winds were cooler. The threat of cyclones and prairie fires was past, and we didn't have to worry about blizzards as yet. Everyone was talking about the County Fair which was scheduled for next week. Together with the usual fall work there was now a bustle of activity to get everything ready for the big event.

Papa was more like himself, his better self, since the fire. He still didn't go out of his way to notice me and rarely spoke directly to me, but he didn't exclude me from conversations either. No one was busier with the Fair than he was. He talked on and on about it and Senator Barker who, he said, would make the opening speech. And he bragged about the good times he would show little Davey.

"He's not even a year old, Sam." Mama reminded him.

"Well, he can ride the merry-go-round with me, can't he?"

If Papa stayed in this good mood, I thought, perhaps all of us would be allowed to go to the Fair. He still hadn't lost his "burr," and we still did morning and evening chores. And sometimes I took the cows to pasture and brought them in at night. My leg was fine now.

We were up before daylight the morning the Fair opened. Our chores were quickly done, breakfast over and dishes washed and the house in order. Vina and Lucy went upstairs to get dressed for the big day. Papa was hitching the greys to the surrey while Mama got dressed and dressed Mae. It was still hard for Vina and me to believe he was letting us go. All of us were ready and waiting when he came in to change.

"Put the stuff you're taking under the back seat, Molly. I'll be

86

ready in a minute." He turned to us. "One thing I want understood, girls. There's to be no shennanigans today. Is that clear?"

"Yes, Papa."

"If I catch any of you making a fool of yourself I'll whale the daylights out of you on the spot. Just you remember that."

"Yes, Papa." If we hadn't agreed he'd have made us stay at home.

Vina whispered to me, "Gee whiz! How can we have any fun with Papa watching us every minute and threatening us with the buggy whip?"

I didn't answer but I was wondering the same thing.

There was a stream of buggies and springwagons and surreys on the road as we drove out our back gate. Thick grey plumes of dust billowed up and rolled away across the prairie.

"Looks like we're going to have a big crowd today," Mama remarked.

"Sure we will. You can bet your bottom dollar every farmer in thirty miles will come with his family. It's not every day they have a chance to see a real live Senator."

The way Mama smiled I thought Papa was joking, or teasing. But he wasn't. "Senator Barker is one of the great men of this state, maybe in the whole country," he said seriously.

Papa had a right, I supposed, to be proud about Senator Barker. It had been mostly through his efforts the Senator was coming to make the opening speech at the Fair. And it was Papa who had persuaded the men from the Agricultural Bureau to act as judges of the livestock entries. He had also insisted a committee from a neighboring county be formed to judge food and garden entries. Judges from Osceola County, he said, might be charged with bias. The Fair Committee finally agreed.

It was not yet nine o'clock when we arrived at the Fairgrounds. Crowds were pouring in through the entrance gate. There was a bandstand just inside, draped with red-white-and-blue bunting. Flags fluttered in the morning breeze. Our local band was playing full blast. Beyond the bandstand was the Midway, lined with booths and long tables, all rapidly filling up with various entries of canned foods, jams and jellies, baked-goods, and fresh garden vegetables. Families from all over the County had brought their best offerings.

To the right of the Midway was a big tent that covered the

merry-go-round. The tinny, monotonous music of the carousel could be heard faintly above the band. Near it was a long narrow tent, open at the front, with shooting galleries and all kinds of games of chance. Papa had told us about such games on the way to the Fair this morning, and warned us about them. They were tricky, he said, and no one ever won anything. "Keep away from 'em!"

Far to the left, removed from the center of excitement, were the corrals for livestock entries.

We gathered inside near the bandstand. Excitement filled the air. We were eager to be a part of it but we had to wait to see what Papa said.

"I'd better make sure everything is set up for Senator Barker," he said importantly. "I'll meet you and the kids here at eleven o'clock, Molly. And *be* here. I don't want any of you to miss the Senator's speech."

"Nor do we want to miss it," Mama said. "Give my regards to the Senator." Papa was already hurrying along the Midway. Mama opened her pocketbook and gave Vina and Lucy and me each a dollar. "I'll keep Mae with me. Hilda and Ethan will be along soon. You girls go on and enjoy yourselves. Just don't spend all your time and money on the merry-go-round. And don't stuff yourselves with cotton candy and popcorn and soda pop. And don't be late." She patted each of us on the shoulder. "I guess that's enough dont's. Run along and have a good time."

There was so much to see and do it was hard to know where to start. But the moment we reached the Midway we were swept along with the crowd toward the merry-go-round. It seemed to be the main attraction.

"Look at that line," Lucy cried as we neared the big tent. "We'll *never* get on!"

"Not if we don't get in line," Vina said. "Come on!"

We held onto each other and pushed out of the Midway crowd; and ran to the end of the line waiting at the ticket booth. It seemed forever before we reached it. One ride cost ten cents, or we could have three for a quarter. We each bought three tickets, then waited in another line to get on. Brightly colored wooden horses with fancy saddles and harness raced around the circle, galloping up and down. Big colored plumes on top of their heads danced to the music.

"Oh, look, Ann! That one's just like Golden," Vina cried. "I'm going to ride it."

"If you get to it first," I said.

Lucy picked a spotted pony and of course I chose a black one with fancy red and gold saddle and bridle. The merry-go-round slowed to a stop. We climbed on and raced to our chosen ponies. As soon as every pony had a rider the conductor started taking tickets. Pretty soon we were moving, faster and faster. Lucy squealed with delight. Vina was singing at the top of her voice. It was easy for me to imagine I was riding Midnight across the prairie with the wind in my face. We stayed on for our three rides and got off reluctantly.

"Let's buy some more tickets," Vina said. "Nothing could be more fun than this."

"How do you know? You haven't seen anything else," I told her. "Let's wander around and come back later." Both agreed.

Jostled by the pushing crowd on the Midway, which was bigger now than before, we finally got to the long tent with its rows of booths. Behind each counter stood a man wearing a straw hat and yelling loudly. "Step right this way! Hurry! Hurry! Hurry! Win a beautiful prize!"

One booth had rows of beautiful dolls on shelves at the back. We stopped to admire them.

"Step right up, little ladies. Win a lovely dolly! Six balls for a quarter. You can't lose!"

"What do we have to do to win?" I asked.

He pointed to a box at the back of the booth with a clown in it. "Just hit him with one of these balls hard enough to knock him out of the box and you got yourself a pretty dolly. It's easy."

"Let me try!" Lucy pleaded.

In spite of Papa's warning we held a whispered conference. It did look easy, and the dolls *were* beautiful. We decided to buy six balls and take turns trying to hit the clown. Whoever knocked the clown from the box got the doll.

Lucy tried first and missed. Vina next, and missed. I did no better. It wasn't as easy as it looked. Now it was Lucy's turn again. This time the ball hit the clown but not hard enough. Vina and I played "eenie, meenie, minie, moe" to decide who got the next throw. I did. My ball didn't even come close.

"Watch me!" Vina said. A crowd had gathered but Vina was too excited to notice. She stepped back, took careful aim and let the ball fly. The clown went through the back of the box. The crowd cheered. The man in the booth didn't look very happy. "Which one?" he asked.

Vina danced up and down trying to decide. "That one! The one with the pink dress."

He handed it to her. "There you are, little lady. You sure got a strong right arm." He took up his spiel again. "Who's next, folks? Step right up! Win a pretty dolly! Anyone can win!"

We pushed our way out of the crowd. Vina held the doll close to protect it.

"How did you do it, Vina?" Lucy wanted to know. "I can throw as well as you can. Why didn't I hit it?"

Vina laughed. "Papa hasn't made *you* throw corn into a wagon. I just told myself that ball was an ear of corn and thought about what Papa would do to me if I missed the wagon."

"Well, *I've* thrown more ears of corn than you have," I said. "And I missed that clown by a mile!"

"Let's do it again," Lucy begged. "Next time I *know* I'll win."

Vina handed the doll to her. "Let's pretend you did."

"You mean I can *have* it! Really, Vina?"

"Sure I mean it. I'd rather ride the merry-go-round. Horses are more fun. Besides, I'm too old for dolls."

Lucy hugged the doll and followed close behind us. We walked on stopping now and then to watch the games at other booths. We didn't try any of them. They looked tricky. Vina had just been lucky to win the doll. No sense tempting our luck. Pretty soon we came to a refreshment stand. The young man behind the counter had on a red-striped suit and straw hat. He was calling in a high-pitched voice, "Popcorn, cracker-jacks, cotton candy, soda pop! Come and get it folks! Only a nickel!"

"He's kinda cute," Vina whispered. "Let's buy something. Mama said we could. I want cotton candy. What do you kids want?"

We bought two sticks of cotton candy and a package of cracker-jacks and shared them. The man winked at Vina when he handed the candy to her, and she smiled.

"Vina, stop flirting! You'll get us all in trouble," I whispered as soon as we were far enough away from the booth. "Remember what Papa said."

"Oh, pooh!" Vina tossed her head and we glanced back to see if the man was still watching her. He was.

We walked away fast. Soon we were back in the Midway crowd again, being pushed along. Where to we couldn't tell. Presently I heard a voice behind me. "Why, hello, Ann!" I turned and saw Nellie Hughes. "I heard about your accident, honey. How are you? Are you alone?" Then she saw Vina and Lucy and smiled. "No, I see you aren't. Isn't the Fair fun? I hope we have one every year, don't you?"

For a second I wondered why Nellie seemed so nervous. Then I saw why. Tom Simpson came up with a stick of cotton candy for her. He didn't see me at first. "Here you are, Nellie. What do you want to do next?"

"Oh, thank you, Tommy dear! You're so good to me." Nellie giggled and linked her arm in his. "Look who's here, Tommy. Ann. She's all right again. Isn't that nice?"

Tom turned and his face got red. He looked so surprised I wanted to laugh but I didn't. "How are you, Tom?"

"I'm . . . I'm fine, Ann. Is your leg really all right?"

"Of course. Broken bones don't stay broken forever, you know. Are you enjoying the Fair?"

"Yes. It's very exciting, don't you think?"

He was trying so hard to get away without being impolite. Poor Tommy! I didn't care that he had brought Nellie to the Fair but he must think I did. I really didn't want him to be so uncomfortable.

"We're having a lot of fun," I said lightly. "We've had three rides on the merry-go-round and Vina won a beautiful doll. There's *so* much to see and do."

Nellie became impatient. "Come on, Tommy, Let's ride the merry-go-round and then maybe you can win *me* a doll. Goodbye, Ann. So glad you're all right." They vanished in the crowd.

I smiled to myself. She didn't care a bit whether I was well again or not. She just wanted to show off. Nellie *was* a lot like Susan!

That made me think of Mr. Evans. He should have arrived at the Fair by this time. I knew he had entered some of his pure-bred stock. Maybe if we wandered over to the corrals we'd run into him.

I don't think I really would have gone looking for him even if we hadn't run into a bunch of kids we knew. They were gathered around the horseshoe pitching contest ground. Gus Gruder and Zeke Simpson were in a hot contest. Each had won a game. Now they were warming up for the third game which would decide the winner. When Gus saw Vina he called out for everyone to hear, "Now I *got* to win! My girl's watching."

Vina blushed and tossed her head as if she hadn't heard or seen him. Gus moved back, squinted at the target, spit on his hands and tossed the horseshoe easily over the peg. The crowd cheered. Now it was Zeke's turn. The shoe landed squarely on top of Gus' horseshoe. The next throw would decide Gus' fate. The crowd was tense and silent. He must have been nervous about Vina watching him. He threw too hard. The horseshoe landed several inches beyond its mark. Now Zeke stepped up to the line. If he missed too, they'd have to play another game. Zeke took his time about throwing, measuring the distance carefully. That horseshoe seemed to float through the air and settle down easily on top of his last one.

The kids cheered and pounded Zeke on the back calling him "The Champion," and telling Gus, "Better luck next time!" Gus was disappointed but a good sport. He grabbed Vina's arm. "Who cares about an old horseshoe game? I got the prettiest girl, anyway! Come on, Vina! Let's *really* see this old Fair."

"You can't go with him, Vina," I whispered. "You know what Papa said."

She gave me her favorite answer, "Oh, pooh!" and went along with Gus. I noticed Sarah Jenkins watching them. She didn't look happy. I think she expected Gus to ask her, and he probably would have if Vina hadn't come along when she did.

The boys began lining up for another game. I took Lucy's hand and started to move away when I saw Will Miller pushing toward us. "You and Lucy alone, Ann? I mean . . ."

"I know what you mean, Willie. No, I didn't come with any special boy. I just want to have fun with everyone today. It's been a long time since I could. Is Elsie here yet, do you know?"

"Oh, sure. They're all with your parents. Everyone is getting ready for Senator Barker's speech."

"But that won't be until eleven."

"I know. We still got time to make the rounds and see what's going on, if you want to. I've had enough horseshoes for one day."

I liked Will. I wondered if he had seen Tom and Nellie together and was trying to make it up to me. I couldn't tell him there was nothing to "make up," that I was happy the way things were. He took Lucy's hand and made a path for us out of the crowd. It seemed to be getting bigger all the time.

It was almost eleven when we got back to the bandstand. Hundreds of people had gathered here for the opening ceremonies. I reached for Lucy's hand. She was clutching the doll with both of them. Suddenly I realized we had to do something with it before we saw Papa. He would be furious about our disobeying him even if we had won. If we could get to the surrey I could hide the doll under the back seat. Papa'd have to know about the doll sometime, but as least hiding it now would postpone our punishment and let us enjoy the Fair. For one day, anyway.

I explained the problem to Will. He understood and took the doll from Lucy. "We'd better put her in the surrey so she won't get crushed in the crowd. You wait here with Ann. I'll be back in a minute or two."

Lucy let go of the doll reluctantly. "I wanted to show her to Mama."

"You can do that later. You don't want her to get broken, do you?" She shook her head. "And let's not say anything about her to Mama or Papa until we get home. Then she'll be a big surprise. All right?"

"I guess so. But I know why Will took the doll. You think Papa will be mad Vina won her, don't you?"

I hugged her. "You're a very smart little girl, honey. We *do* want to keep Papa in a good mood, don't we?"

"Would he make us go home if he knew about the doll?"

"He might. And that would make Mama unhappy."

"I won't say anything. I can keep a secret."

Will came back. We finally found Mama and Papa. Elsie

93

and Jed and Davey were with them. So were Uncle Ethan, Aunt Hilda and Hans and Kathy. But Vina wasn't there.

"Where is Vina?" was Mama first question.

I couldn't tell her in front of Papa. If he knew she'd gone off with Gus he'd skin her alive! Or threaten to. "She'll be along in a minute. We ran into Nellie Hughes."

"Well, I hope she'll get here in time for the speech. It's almost eleven."

So did I. But not with Gus Gruder!

Papa looked at his watch. "Time for me to get up to the speaker's platform. I'll meet you all after the ceremonies."

As soon as he was out of hearing I started to tell Mama about Vina. Before I could get her attention there was a loud roll of drums. The crowd quieted. Only the sing-song music of the carousel could be heard distantly. Officials of the Fair, Judges from the Agricultural Bureau, and Senator Barker already were seated on the platform. Bert Jenkins, Chairman of the Fair Committee stepped up behind the flag-draped podium and waited for quiet. He spoke briefly, welcoming everyone to Osceola County's first Fair. When he sat down Papa came to the podium. He spoke in a loud, clear voice.

"And now, Ladies and Gentlemen, we come to the point in these opening ceremonies I know you have all been waiting for." He paused. "It is an honor and a privilege to bring before you today a man whose name and deeds are acclaimed throughout the length and breadth of our fair State. A man who grew up right here in Osceola County, whose untiring efforts and brilliant statesmanship have done so much to make Iowa a great State, and Osceola County the best place *in* this great State to live and bring up our children." Again he paused. "Ladies and Gentlemen, it is with heartfelt pride I now present to you Senator James W. Barker."

The crowd went wild with applause. Senator Barker waited, smiling, until they quieted down, then began his speech. "Thank you all. It is a great pleasure, indeed, to be here with you today . . ."

I didn't hear much of his speech. I was too worried about Vina. She still hadn't come. If she weren't back by the time the speech was finished we'd all be in for it. Fortunately Mama was listening to Senator Barker and hadn't noticed Vina's absence.

The speech was almost over when Vina slipped through the crowd and touched me on the shoulder. "Did they miss me?" she whispered.

I stepped back out of Mama's hearing. "Of course they did, silly! Where have you been? You know what you're in for if Papa finds out you were with Gus."

"I'll tell you about it later," she whispered, her eyes dancing. Then she noticed Lucy didn't have the doll. "Where's the doll?"

"We hid it in the surrey. Lucy promised not to say anything about it."

"You think of everything, don't you. Thanks!" She squeezed my hand and moved in behind Mama as if she had been there all the time.

Senator Barker finished speaking and sat down. The applause went on for quite a while, then the crowd began to scatter. Most everyone was heading for the picnic grounds. Papa came down from the platform and joined us.

Uncle Ethan said, "That was a fine introduction, Sam. And a fine speech from the Senator. I hope he meant what he said about better roads."

"He sure does. I've been harping about them for four years now. With Senator Barker pushing for 'em, we'll get them."

"I don't agree with him on State help, though. That sounds like vote-getting oratory. Farmers don't want handouts. We've taken care of our problems right well up to now without 'em."

"I'm with you on that," Papa agreed. "Still, if we had more men like Senator Barker ready to put through more legislature *in favor* of the farmers a lot of things would be better for everybody."

Papa talked like he knew the Senator real well. Mama said he had never met him until he went to see him about speaking at the Fair. "It's not how long you've known a man, honey. It's how well you understand him. Papa and Senator Barkley understand each other quite well."

All the way to the picnic grounds people kept stopping to tell him what a great thing he had done bringing the Senator to open the Fair and what a great speech he had made. Papa was very pleased with himself and in a good mood. That mattered very much to all of us.

Long tables had been set up at the edge of the Fairgrounds.

Over some, lengths of canvas, supported by ten-foot poles, provided shade. We spread our checkered tablecloths on one of the unprotected tables and unpacked the picnic baskets. Fried chicken, potato salad, deviled eggs, pickles and cole-slaw, with plenty of bread-and-butter sandwiches. There were several kinds of pies and cakes and watermelon and muskmelon from Uncle Ethan's prize patch.

"We might as well just camp here for three days," Mama laughed. "We've certainly got enough food."

"Ja!" Aunt Hilda said. "Kids un' papas hungry like bears."

"This papa sure is," Papa said. "I could eat a whole crock of that chicken by myself."

"Not if I get there first," Uncle Ethan chuckled.

All around us other families were unpacking baskets, calling greetings to neighbors. Hans and Kathy had Davey between them. "Look, Mama! Davey can walk now just like us," Hans cried.

"Ja. Davey big boy now. Take him to his mama un' come sit."

We had just finished heaping our plates when I saw Mr. Evans. Papa must have seen him about the same time. "Jim! Over here!" he called. "Come join us. We've got plenty of food."

He threaded a path through the crowd and looked down at our feast. "You certainly have, and it looks mighty delicious. I'm tempted to stay, but I promised Mrs. Hughes I'd join her family. That is, if I can find them. This is quite a crowd. Where did all the people come from anyway?"

"A lot of them are from neighboring counties," Papa told him, adding, "You sure you won't change your mind and stay where you *know* there's food, Jim?"

He laughed. "It might be a good idea, at that. But I did promise. I'll have another look around. If I don't find the Hugheses I'll be back — if I'm still invited."

"The invitation stands," Mama assured him. "I can't guarantee how much food will be left."

"I'll take that chance." He came over to where I was sitting, and leaned down, speaking in a loud whisper. "Do you think you could save me a piece of that coconut cake, Ann?"

"I'll save you two pieces," I whispered loudly. Everyone laughed.

He must have found the Hugheses. He didn't come back. After a while Papa got up and picked up Davey. "We're going for a merry-go-round ride."

"Oh, Papa, he hasn't had his nap," Elsie protested.

"He doesn't need a nap. Davey's a big boy now. He wants to ride the horseys with Grandpa, don't you, son?" He swung him up onto his shoulders. He clung to Papa's neck. "Hold tight, now! Here we go!" He galloped off across the grounds with Davey shouting in glee.

They'd been gone about fifteen minutes when Mr. Evans came back. Rev. Pritchard was with him. "I've generously agreed to share my cake with Martin, Ann," he announced, smiling. "That is, if you were able to save *two* pieces. Otherwise, Martin, you're out of luck."

Mama had spread a cloth over the left-over food. She lifted one corner and took out the coconut cake. "You're both in luck. It seems everyone else preferred chocolate." Almost half of the coconut cake was left. "See if there is some coffee left, Ann." She divided the remaining cake in two generous slabs. There was enough coffee for two full cups.

"You should have entered *this* cake in the baking contest, Mrs. Bullard," Rev. Pritchard exclaimed after the first bite. "Though I must say I'm glad you didn't. It's delicious." Mr. Evans agreed enthusiastically.

"She did enter one just like it," I told them.

"Then it's sure to take first prize," Rev. Pritchard said. He finished his piece of cake and turned to me. "We've missed you at church, Ann. I'm glad you were able to be here today. Are you enjoying the Fair?"

"Oh, very much. What I've seen of it, that is. I certainly enjoyed the merry-go-round."

"Would you believe it, Ann, I haven't been on a merry-go-round for so long I'd probably fall off the horse at the first turn," he laughed.

"No, I wouldn't believe it! I mean, that you'd fall off the horse."

"I hope you're not going to ask me to prove it," he said, pretending to be worried. "Several of my congregation might consider such behavior most unseemly for a minister."

I laughed. "I know just which members you mean, too!"

Suddenly Mama exclaimed, "My goodness! It's almost two o'clock. The baked-goods judging starts at two thirty." She started gathering up the food.

"You go on with Aunt Hilda, Mama. We'll take care of things here. And don't worry," Elsie said.

"May we go back to the Fair then, Mama?" Vina asked.

"Yes, but stay out of mischief. And make sure you're back at the surrey by ten minutes to five."

Mr. Evans and Rev. Pritchard carried the packed baskets to our surrey, then left for the livestock corrals. Elsie and Jed came with us. Mama had taken Mae with her. She was still too little to do so much walking. Vina whispered to me, "I promised to meet Gus at the lemonade stand. That's why I was late for Senator Baker's speech. Gus was trying to win one of those pretty parasols for me. He wouldn't give up. Honestly, I think Papa was right. Some of those games *are* dishonest. But Gus kept saying if I could win something, he *had* to. And went right on playing no matter how many times he lost."

"You can't meet him, Vina. You know Papa took Davey to the merry-go-round. If he sees you with Gus you know what will happen."

"That's *why* I have to meet him. To tell him about Papa. Then maybe he'll stop spending all his money on those silly games."

"All right. But don't go near the merry-go-round."

"Don't worry! There are lots of things to see." And as soon as we got into the crowd, she disappeared.

We found Papa and Davey at the carousel. Papa was on a big white horse with Davey in the saddle in front of him. He waved to us as they whirled by. Jed bought tickets for all of us. "What happened to Vina?"

"Oh, she went to meet some of the kids at the lemonade stand."

Elsie looked concerned. "All right. But if Papa asks where she is we'd better let him think she is with Mama."

The merry-go-round stopped and we climbed on. Papa insisted upon keeping Davey "for just one more ride". He didn't even notice Vina wasn't with us.

It was after three when we left the merry-go-round and started back to the Midway. And ran into Mr. Evans. "I was looking for you, Sam. Ethan wants us to meet him over at the livstock show."

Elsie took Davey from Papa. He turned to Jed. "Why don't you come, too, son? Livestock's more interesting than a bunch of women gabbing about pies and cakes. The girls can get back to the Midway without you."

"Go along, Jed," Elsie told him. "We *will* be all right."

We were nearing the baked-goods booth on the Midway before I remembered Vina wasn't with us. Mama would ask questions even if Papa wasn't there to ask them. "I'd better try to find her. You know how she is, no sense of time when she's having a good time. If Papa finds out . . . ."

"Who knows better than I what he'll do," Elsie laughed. "Oh, I can laugh about it now because I'm happy with Jed and Davey. But it wasn't funny then. It's not right, Ann, for Papa to keep you kids tied down the way he did me. Maybe it was necessary for everyone to work that hard when we first came here but it certainly isn't now. By the way, what happened between you and Tom? He brought Nellie Hughes to the Fair and he's been buggy-riding with her several times, I hear."

"Nothing happened. I never had any strings on Tom, or he on me."

"I thought you liked him. He was sure mighty attentive to you."

"I do. But we're just friends. At least we were until Papa scared him half to death with all those accusations after my accident. I don't blame Tom for avoiding me now. All he did that day was try to help and Papa hit him and then ordered him off the place, practically calling him a liar."

"No one but Papa ever thought there was anything more than friendship between you two. I doubt Papa believed it himself. He just wanted something to rant around about."

"That didn't keep him from punishing me for something I didn't do. I'm surprised he let any of us come to the Fair."

"Maybe you can thank Senator Barker for that," Elsie laughed. "Go on now, and find Vina before she gets into trouble. But just between us, I hope she *is* with Gus!"

I turned back toward the merry-go-round and lemonade stand. It was nice to talk with Elsie alone. We had so few chances lately. And she had changed. But in a nice way because she was so happy. She was only interested now in her home and family. Sometimes when I tried to talk to her about a book I had just finished and liked very much, she would listen a while then I'd notice she was getting restless and usually would find something she had to do right away. I wondered if she had completely forgotten the things we used to dream about. Did this happen to every girl when she got married?

These were not thoughts for a happy day, I told myself. I pushed through the crowd around the merry-go-round looking for Vina. Shrill tinny whistles and shouting voices deafened me. How could I ever find Vina in this mob? Maybe I should look at the games booths. Yes, that was where she most likely was. Either watching Gus lose his money or trying to get him to stop. I turned, and bumped head-on into Rev. Pritchard.

"Ann! What are you doing here by yourself?" He took my arm and protected me from the shoving crowd.

"I'm looking for Vina."

"Is she lost? I mean did you get separated?"

"Not exactly." I couldn't tell him the whole truth. "She went to meet some of the other kids. I've got to find them."

"You're not likely to in this crowd. Let's get out of it and try somewhere else. Perhaps they're at the lemonade stand."

The crowd around the lemonade stand was worse. Rev. Pritchard stood on a bench and looked for Vina. "I don"t see her," he said, stepping down. "Who would be with her?"

I hesitated. "Well, maybe Gus and Sarah and . . . and Will. I don't really know." This wasn't a lie. Vina might very well be with some of the kids, including Gus.

He stepped up on the bench again and searched the crowd, then stepped down. "If they were here I'd certainly have seen one or two of them. You look tired, Ann. Let me find a seat for you and get you a lemonade. When you're rested we'll both look for Vina and her friends."

I welcomed the rest. My leg was hurting a little and my throat was dry as a corn-cob. I'd probably have to tell him the whole truth about Vina, but that could wait.

"That place is more crowded than my church on Sunday," he laughed when he handed me the cup of lemonade. He sat down and took a deep breath. "It *does* feel good to sit for a while. Do they always have such crowds at these Fairs?"

"I don't know. This is the first one they've had since we moved here. I think it's the first one they've ever had."

He said seriously, "And they probably wouldn't have had this one if your father hadn't kept after all of us and persuaded Senator Barker to come here. It's a strange thing, Ann. An outsider often makes us see things a neighbor couldn't. For instance, your father. He's been arguing for better roads ever since I came here and probably before that. But it took Senator Barker to wake us up. Oh, I know he was born in the County but still he's an outsider in a way. I've been button-holed by three local citizens this afternoon on the subject of roads. You'd think, to hear them, it was *their* idea." He stopped suddenly "Forgive me, Ann. I didn't mean to preach a sermon. Would you like another lemonade?"

"Oh, no, thank you. But I did enjoy it." My voice sounded strange and I suddenly felt clumsy and confused. Rev. Pritchard had never looked at me the way he was doing today. Like he was seeing me and nothing else. Still, I was pleased by the things he had said about Papa. Maybe we girls *were* too close to him to see his best qualities.

"Is Vina really lost, Ann?" he asked abruptly.

Goodness! Did he think I would lie to *him?* Maybe I had twisted the truth a little, but that was all.

"I mean," he went on, "are you sure you aren't just being a big sister and worrying needlessly?"

He was probably right but I couldn't admit it. Now that I thought about it, I *didn't* have any real reason to believe Vina was lost or into mischief. She may be with Mama at the Midway. "Maybe I am, a little," I told him. "But Vina does forget about time when she's having fun and Papa's very strict about punctuality. I don't want her to be late and get scolded." If a scolding had been *all* she was in for it wouldn't have been so bad!

"It is good to think of others, Ann. Good for them and good for us. But we can over-do it, you know. Sometimes we deprive others of experiences they need in order to learn valuable lessons. Even painful experiences often have a good purpose." He stopped. "There I go, preaching again! When all I really wanted to say was that you should be enjoying the Fair, not

101

worrying about Vina. Why don't we see some of the exhibits together?"

"I'd like that. I'm not tired now. And Vina *is* probably all right." Papa couldn't object if he saw me with Rev. Pritchard. And it might be fun seeing the Fair with him. I *hadn't* seen much of it so far.

"What would you like to see first? We've almost two hours before they start closing."

"I must be back at the surrey before five. Mama's orders. But I would like very much to see the horses." Neither of us mentioned that I no longer had one of my own. Perhaps he didn't know that.

He took my arm and we walked slowly past the "strip" where the games were. The crowds were beginning to thin out. The games were still going at a lively pace and I kept an eye out for Vina. She wasn't there. I hoped she would remember and be back on time, but I wasn't going to worry about her.

The crowd had not thinned, it seemed, around the livestock exhibits. We had to push our way through to get close enough to see. What magnificent horses! I leaned on the fence wondering which one I'd pick if Papa really would let me have another one of my own.

He seemed to read my thoughts. "Which one do you like, Ann?"

"I don't know. They're all so beautiful. Yes I do! The black one over there, with the white star on his forehead."

"He's probably pretty expensive."

I laughed. "Do you know about horses *too*, Rev. Pritchard?"

"Not very much, I'm afraid, but you can usually spot a thoroughbred. There's just something about them that is different. People as well as animals."

I was sure now that he did know I no longer had Midnight. I could talk freely. "Papa wouldn't let me have another horse of my own anyway. So there's no use wishing."

"On the contrary, my dear! Wishing is *mighty* important." He sounded so much like Mr. Evans I glanced up to see if he was really serious. There was a twinkle in his eyes.

I laughed. "Very well! I'll wish as hard as I can, and we'll see. It didn't do any good when I wished we didn't have to live on a farm."

"Do you still wish that?"

"Not exactly. Maybe wishes change as you get older. I love the farm now, especially in the spring and autumn. I like riding across the prairie at sundown to bring the cows in. And I love watching the leaves turn after the first frost. But I *don't* like Mama working so hard, and our having to wade through snow-drifts to get to school." It was a long speech for me and I was suddenly embarrassed.

He didn't seem to notice. "You like school, don't you?"

"Oh, very much. More than ever since Miss Engles came. She's so beautiful, and very wise, too. Don't you agree?"

He smiled. "You're very pretty yourself, Ann. Don't you know that?"

He didn't wait for me to answer. He took his watch from his pocket and exclaimed. "My goodness! I can't believe it's after four! I'd better get you back to the surrey or I'll be in trouble with your mother." He smiled and took my arm.

We circled the exhibit trying to avoid the crowd. I was surprised not to see Papa or Mr. Evans or Uncle Ethan. Jed had probably left to meet Elsie.

"This has been a very pleasant occasion for me, Ann. I hope I didn't bore you with my lectures." He laughed softly. "That's the trouble with preachers. They never know when to stop preaching."

"I didn't think you were preaching. I like talking the way we have this afternoon, about life and people and . . ." I stopped. I wanted to tell him he wasn't at all stuffy the way people seemed to expect a preacher to be, but he was looking at me in that strange way again, as if he'd never seen me before.

We went back to the Midway. The baked-goods contest was over when we reached Mama's booth. And sure enough, Vina was there with the rest of the family, except Papa. Mama's coconut cake had won a prize, but first prize had gone to Aunt Hilda's sour cream chocolate cake.

"I'm not the least bit surprised, ladies," Rev. Pritchard said gallantly. "I tasted that coconut cake — a rather big taste I might add, and . . ."

"My cake you not taste yet!" Aunt Hilda interrupted. "Come home *mit* us for supper. Another cake I got, joost like prize one."

Rev. Pritchard laughed. "I *really* wasn't hinting, Mrs. Stone."

"Ja! Ja!, Hilda know." She moved closer and whispered. "I vud ask you anyway."

Rev. Pritchard left with Aunt Hilda and her children. Uncle Ethan would be waiting for them at the hitching post. Elsie and Vina went on ahead, Vina carrying Davey piggy-back. At last I had a chance to speak to Mama alone. I didn't say anything about going to the livestock show with Rev. Pritchard. I only told her about the doll Vina had won and given to Lucy. "I hid it under the back seat, Mama."

"Papa told you not to play those games, Ann. He's going to be pretty upset when he learns you disobeyed him. And he *will* learn of it."

"You won't tell him, will you? Do you have to, Mama?"

"I won't need to tell him. He'll know when he sees the doll, won't he?"

"Yes. But Vina *did* win. The games can't all be tricky. Won't that make a difference?"

"I hope so, dear."

Luckily Papa didn't find out about the doll until long after the Fair was over and by that time so much had happened the doll no longer was important.

# CHAPTER IX
## 1895

Supper that night was more like the good times before my accident. Papa was expansive and jovial. He had a right to feel pleased about the Fair. It had been his idea from the beginning. Most of it anyway. Certainly the success of the first day was a triumph for him. All during supper he talked about the things Senator Barker had said, in his speech and to him personally, and how pleased the Committee was about everything.

Listening to him — and there was not much choice — I remembered the nice things Rev. Pritchard had said about Papa and my own reflections on them. Maybe we didn't always understand him. But for now it was enough that he was happy and was letting us be happy too in our own way. At least some of the time!

"I think I'll have another piece of that pie, Molly. And another cup of coffee. A man can sure work up an appetite traipsing around those fairgrounds." He chuckled to himself. "Danged if I ever realized before how *much* ground they cover!"

Mama brought the pie and coffee and offered us another piece of cake. We were too full to eat all of the first piece. It was just as well Papa did all the talking.

"And that Davey!" he went on. "More energy than a young steer. He's going to be a real horseman, Molly. Any other kid his age would have been scared to death on the merry-go-round, screamed his head off. Not Davey! He grabbed the reins and sat up straight as you please. The faster we went the more he liked it." Now for the first time since we got home he seemed to notice us. "What did you kids do all day?"

Vina spoke up quickly. "Oh, we rode the merry-go-round, watched the horseshoe pitching contest, and just wandered around. It was a lot of fun, Papa."

"How did you make out, Ann. Leg give you any trouble?" The question and his concern took me by surprise. It was the first time he had mentioned the accident since the day after it happened. And the first time he had spoken directly to me in all these weeks.

"No trouble, Papa. I think it's all right now. Good as new, like Dr. Matthews said it would be." Wanting to please him I added. "I enjoyed Senator Barker's speech." As soon as I said it I felt ashamed. I hadn't heard a word of the speech because of Vina. But Papa *was* pleased.

"We don't get much chance out here to listen to great men. You kids can be mighty proud you heard Senator Barker today. There's not a more important man in the whole State of Iowa."

"Has he gone back to the capital?" Mama asked.

"Of course. He's a busy man. He's come a long way since he helped his father farm on homesteaded land not twenty miles from here. A lot of people depend upon him." He finished the pie and pushed back his plate. "I better fix that back fence while there's some daylight left. Won't be time to do it tomorrow."

Lucy had been quiet all through supper. "Are we going to the Fair tomorrow, Papa?" It was the question the rest of us hadn't the courage to ask. We waited for his answer.

"Not all of us. I've *got* to go. I'm on the Committee. And Mama has to be there for the judgings. You girls will just have to stay here and look after things. Cyrus can't do everything, and farm work won't wait for a county fair. Those root crops have to be dug and stored before frost. And you know there's still corn to be harvested. Vina can help Cy. Ann and Lucy can get started on the root crops."

Mama protested. "Oh, Sam! *Two days* won't make that much difference. Let the children enjoy the Fair with the rest of us. They've earned it."

"It's not a question of what they've earned, Molly. And two days can make a big difference this time of year. First thing you know snow will be flying and it'll be too late to dig the root crops."

"Sam! This is September! At least another month before we get snow."

"You can't be sure about that. No sense putting it off and being sorry when it's too late. Besides, the kids have had a whole day at the Fair."

I suppose Mama realized it would do no good to argue or

protest further. Whether we, or Mama, liked it or not, the Fair was over for us. Papa still had his "burr." His concern about my leg was just to find out how much work I was able to do now!

Papa left the house. Vina and Lucy began to complain. "It's not fair, Mama!" Vina cried, almost in tears. "I've worked like a horse for weeks. And besides, he said himself I saved the crops in the prairie fire. Why can't I have some fun now? What can I tell my friends?"

"You can tell them we have the *meanest* Papa in the whole world!" Lucy said.

Mae began to cry. "I want to ride the merry-go-round!"

"Hush! All of you," Mama scolded. "I don't agree with Papa about this but he is your father. I expect you to act your age, not behave like babies. I'll talk with him tonight. If I can't make him change his mind, I'm afraid you'll just have to do as he says. Missing the rest of the Fair won't be the end of the world. There will be other County Fairs."

For her sake we said no more. We knew she would stay at home with us if she didn't have to go for the judgings.

Vina and I washed the dishes and went upstairs before Papa came back. "It's a good thing he didn't see you with Gus," I told her. "He'd have had a real excuse for making us stay home."

"We're being punished anyway, aren't we? What does it matter whether he has an excuse or not?"

"You'd have gotten a whipping too if he'd seen you."

"I wouldn't care if he had. I'll show him! I'll wait 'til he leaves tomorrow and go to the Fair anyway. I'll go with Mama. Even if he sees me he can't do anything about it. He wouldn't want all those people to know how mean he really is!"

"But *you'd really* catch it when you got home. And so would Mama for letting you go when he said you couldn't."

"I've *got* to go, Ann! I promised Gus I'd meet him. How can I explain to him why I didn't keep my promise? Nobody would believe Papa is as mean as he is unless they saw it with their own eyes. What good is it to be rich if you never have any fun?" She stormed around the room, her black eyes snapping.

"Stop prancing, Vina! You're acting just like Papa when he

107

gets mad. Besides, you're wearing out our carpet. And we *aren't* rich."

She sat down on the side of the bed but her anger hadn't cooled much. "I'll run away, that's what I'll do! I *won't* go on working like a boy just because we haven't any brothers!"

"It's not as bad as it used to be, Vina. Papa *has* changed a little." I told her what Mama had said about the burr in Papa's blanket. Soon we were both laughing.

"At least he didn't find the doll," Vina gloated.

We had solved that problem on the way home from the Fair by putting the doll in one of the empty lunch baskets. While Papa unhitched the team we carried in the things from the surrey and took the doll to Lucy's room. Mama didn't entirely approve of our deception but she agreed there was no point in upsetting Papa. There was no way we could undo what we had done anyway. But our worry over the doll and the reception had been useless. No more fun at the Fair for us. Only long hours of hard work until school started. And that was more than a month away.

As soon as we heard the screen door slam we kept quiet. Maybe Mama *would* be able to change his mind about the Fair. For a while there was only the scraping of a chair on the kitchen floor and the creak of it as Papa sat down. This was a sound we knew well. Then there was the squashy sound the bread made when Mama kneaded it.

"I saved the supper coffee, Sam, if you want a cup," she said. Papa was always easier to handle when he had a cup of coffee in front of him.

"I sure do. There's a real nip in the air tonight. Wouldn't surprise me if we had an early frost this year."

Vina whispered. "Doesn't sound too good for us!"

There was silence for a while, then Mama went on talking but too low for us to hear. Papa's replies were garbled by swallows of coffee. Then suddenly he raised his voice. "That's what comes of letting you get the reins in the first place! A man's a fool to let that happen with any woman. I'll swear, Molly, I wish your father'd never left you a cent of that money!"

Mama spoke up. "You might be swearing more if he hadn't," she said calmly.

"There you go, throwing it up to me! *Your* money saved

108

the old homestead. *Your* money saved the hardware store. *Your* money bought all this fancy furniture. And your money, Molly Bullard, is making weaklings of those girls. They're getting so impudent there's no living with them. Traipsing off with any boy . . ."

"Stop it, Sam! Right now!" Mama was no longer calm. "I don't know what has got into you tonight but you're not taking it out on the children, *or* me. And if I didn't know you're going to be sorry tomorrow for what you've said we'd all walk out of this house tonight! You've got to stop blaming Ann for that accident, and working Vina half to death."

"I'm not talking about the accident. It's what those kids had been up to *before* I'm concerned about."

"You know as well as I do they hadn't been 'up to' anything, if you wen't too stubborn to admit it."

Papa was silenced by that for a while. "Well, you can call it stubborn if you want to. I say it's discipline. And these kids are going to be disciplined one way or another. To start with they're *not* going to the Fair tomorrow. And from now on they're going to do what they're told or get a tanning."

Mama always seemed to know when it was best to let him have the last word. For the time being! She said quietly, "You'd better get to bed." Papa couldn't go on quarreling by himself. Pretty soon we heard footsteps on the stairs. We got into bed quickly and blew out the lamp.

"Well, that settled *our* fate," Vina whispered. "The *slaves* better get some sleep 'fore 'ole massa' starts cracking the whip!"

I agreed. But Mama hadn't had the last word yet. There was still hope.

Papa had had his breakfast and was gone when we came down the next morning. The first thing Vina said was, "Did you talk to Papa about the Fair?" pretending we hadn't heard most of what had been said.

"We still say good-morning in this house, young lady!"

"I'm sorry, Mama. It was just . . ."

"I know. But there's no cause to forget your manners. As for the Fair, I'm afraid I wasn't persuasive enough this time. We'll have to make the best of it for the present. Eat your breakfast, both of you."

We ate the hot oatmeal without really tasting it, or wanting it, then put on our work clothes.

"The judgings won't be until afternoon. I'll have a hot meal for you when you come in at noon. Elsie will come by for me in plenty of time."

"Has Papa left for the Fairgrounds?" Vina asked.

"Not yet. He'll be in soon to change. So go along, now. And girls, you don't have to do *all* the work in one day, remember." She was smiling.

Cy was waiting in the back yard with the wagon. Vina climbed up on the seat with him. Lucy and I headed for the potato field.

It was a clear, beautiful morning, but the sun already was warm. It promised to be unseasonably hot. A nice day for the Fair, but *not* for digging potatoes. As we stooped over the long rows we talked about the fun we'd had yesterday. Maybe Mama would be able to persuade Papa to let us go one more time. I hoped Vina would be able to make Gus understand about today. I wondered if he would wait for her at the lemonade stand. Probably about as long as Tom had waited for me!

By noon we had several baskets of plump dirt-crusted potatoes ready for storing. Hot and tired, Lucy and I washed up on the back porch, ate and rested a while at Mama's insistence. As we were leaving for the field again Elsie drove up. Davey was with her but Jed wasn't. He would meet them later at the Fairgrounds.

"I really shouldn't be going myself," she said. "There's so much to do at the farm right now. But Papa would be disappointed if I didn't bring Davey. And so would Davey. All morning he's been bouncing up and down in his high-chair, gurgling  Go! Go! Go!"

We talked a while then watched them drive away. Walking back to the potato field neither of us said anything. Lucy was probably feeling as sorry for herself as I was.

We had been digging for a couple of hours when I heard the commotion and saw that it was at the house. A springwagon and two buggies had turned in at the back gate. I watched as two men jumped out of one of the buggies and hurried to the springwagon. Then they lifted something from it and went toward the house. Mama and Aunt Hilda got out of the other

110

buggy and hurried in ahead of the men. The man on the spring-wagon picked up Mae, Elsie carried Davey. They went inside.

I yelled to Lucy at the other end of the row. "Someone's hurt."

We ran all the way to the house. Aunt Hilda and Mae, and Elsie with Davey in her lap, were in the kitchen. Their faces were wet with tears.

"What's wrong? What happened?" I asked in a whisper, and looked from Aunt Hilda to Elsie. "Where is Mama?"

No one answered. Lucy went to Elsie and put her arms around her. Elsie was crying. It seemed forever before Aunt Hilda came and put her arms around me. "It's your papa. He's hurt. Real bad. Your mama mit him." Uncle Ethan and Will also were upstairs in the bedroom. Mr. Hughes had gone to the Jenkins farm to get Dr. Matthews. Was Mr. Jenkins hurt too, I wondered? Tears filled my eyes.

It seemed a very long time before Mama and Uncle Ethan and Will came downstairs. Their faces were drawn and anxious. "We've done all we can do, Molly," Uncle Ethan was saying. "We'll just have to wait for Dr. Matthews. Sam probably won't regain consciousness for a while. At least he won't feel the pain."

All of us were silent. Aunt Hilda made Mama sit down and started fixing some coffee. The men found chairs. Lucy took Mae onto her lap. I went to Mama and put my arms around her. She leaned against me, crying softly. Lucy and I still didn't know how Papa had been hurt. No one wanted to talk about it. I wished Dr. Matthews would hurry. When he finally got here Mama and Uncle Ethan went upstairs with him. The rest of us waited in the kitchen.

At last they came back downstairs. Dr. Matthews set his bag on the table and Mama told all of us to sit down. She wanted us to hear what Dr. Matthews had to say about Papa. It was hard to believe the things he said. He told us Papa had considerable damage to the spine. How serious or how permanent it might be he couldn't tell until Papa regained consciousness.

"There could be internal injuries too. He's not hemorrhaging and that's a good sign. Probably only a torn ligament. But he must not be moved or allowed to move. That's very important."

He had strapped Papa to the bed and given him an injection to make him sleep. He'd probably sleep all night, he said, but someone must stay by him to make sure he didn't move in his sleep.

"If he comes to, just keep him quiet. I'll be back first thing in the morning. Maybe I can tell more about his condition then."

Aunt Hilda brought him a cup of coffee. There were so many questions I wanted to ask. Why didn't someone tell us what had happened? Dr. Matthews finished the coffee and got up. "You know how sorry I am about this, Mrs. Bullard. But he's alive and he has a good chance of recovery. We must be thankful for that. Sam's a strong man, and we'll do everything we possibly can to help him." He picked up his bag and went to the door.

Mama went with him. "Thank you for all you've done, Doctor. And for not trying to spare our feelings. It's best we know how serious it is. I'll stay by him all night, of course."

"Let someone else do that, Mrs. Bullard. You need rest, too. You've had a terrible shock. He's likely to be unconscious for several hours, so rest while you can."

Mama finally agreed to lie down in my room where she could hear if Papa made the slightest sound. Aunt Hilda would take Mae home with her and get Mrs. Hughes to stay with the children, then come back and stay the night at our house. Will would drive Elsie and Davey home and get Jed in from the field. He'd come back here to help with the stock.

Elsie was still tearful when she left. "I'll be over early in the morning, Mama. If you need Will and me before then send Vina to get us."

Vina! Good heavens, she was still with Cy in the cornfield!

"We'll drive by and tell them," Uncle Ethan said. "And Ann, be sure your mama rests as long as she can. Hilda will be back in about an hour."

Lucy and I were alone now in the kitchen. It seemed a long time ago that Papa had sat at this table telling Mama we couldn't go to the Fair. Now he was upstairs, maybe dying. How we had hated him this morning! Now we would have given up almost anything to see him come walking down the stairs. I thought of what Vina had said. She would feel guilty and ashamed now. She was always sorry for things she said when angry. I thought of the "burr" in Papa's blanket, and that Mama had said maybe sometime he would stand still long

112

enough for someone to help him. Poor Papa! Now he would have to *lie* still. I wondered if this were God's way of making him accept help. It seemed like a pretty harsh way, but then Papa was a very stubborn man. I was sure God knew that.

Lucy was the first to speak. "How did Papa get hurt, Ann?"

"I don't know any more than you do. Mama will tell us when she gets up. Vina should be here soon."

Vina came in on tiptoe. Her face was streaked with tears. She threw herself into my arms. sobbing. "Oh, Ann, what happened? He won't die will he?"

Her crying must have awakened Mama. She came downstairs and gathered us around her. "Papa's going to be all right, darlings. Dr. Matthews will know what to do when he comes tomorrow. Now we must let him sleep."

She gave us a handkerchief and we dried our tears. "How did it happen, Mama?" I asked.

She looked at me strangely for a moment. "That's right, you weren't there! I forgot about that. You three *don't* know what happened."

"No, Mama. But don't talk about it now if you don't want to. Dr. Matthews said you should rest."

"I'm all right, dear. It all happened so fast. The noise, the frightened horses, and . . . . ." She was silent for a while trying to remember it all clearly. Her voice was choked as she told us about it.

Elsie had told Papa she would bring Davey to the Fair and leave him there with Papa for the rest of the day. When they arrived at the meeting place Papa was talking with some men and didn't see them drive up. Elsie went to get him leaving Mama and Davey in the buggy. Papa and Elsie had almost reached the buggy when the calliope started up with a loud blast. The horses reared, jerking the reins from Mama's hands, and started to run. Elsie screamed. Papa lunged and grabbed the bridle of the horse nearest him. The frightened animals plunged on, dragging Papa until he fell. The buggy wheels rolled over him. Someone finally stopped the horses. Mama and Davey were all right, but Papa lay bleeding and unconscious where he had fallen.

Mama was crying now. "If he hadn't held on as long as

113

he did the buggy would have overturned. Davey and I might have been killed. It's a miracle Papa wasn't."

None of us said anything. There was nothing we could say to comfort her or ourselves. It was still possible Papa *had* given his life to save Mama and Davey. Papa might not get well. Even Dr. Matthews hadn't sounded very sure. I thought of all the times Elsie and I had hated him so much we wanted him to die. Now I prayed silently that he would live. I promised God and myself never to hate him again no matter what he did to me. In my heart I forgave him for selling our horses and for all the mean things he had said to Vina and me. I prayed God would forgive him too, and let him live.

Aunt Hilda came back. Only Mama's deep faith made possible the long hours of waiting. Willingly now, with contrite hearts, Lucy and I went back to the potato field. Cy wouldn't let Vina go back to the cornfield so she came with us. In doing our work maybe we were helping Papa in the only way we could.

Dr. Matthews came early the next morning as promised. Sometime during the night Papa had regained consciousness. Dr. Matthews and Mama went upstairs while Aunt Hilda made breakfast. We waited anxiously .They were upstairs a long time, and when finally they came down Mama's face was very pale.

"I know you want the truth, Mrs. Bullard." He glanced at us sitting at the table. "Are you sure . . . ."

"Yes. Whatever it is the children should know too."

"I'm afraid the injury to the spine is severe. Right now his legs are paralyzed. How permanently only time and care can determine. Fortunately the internal injuries are less serious. Rest and medication and proper nourishment will repair these. But the vertebrae are badly crushed. Only an xray can tell us whether the nerves are permanently damaged. As soon as he can be moved, maybe in a week or two, we'll have to get him to Sioux City."

"If the nerves *are* destroyed . . . . .?"

Dr. Matthews put his hand on her shoulder. "Let's not worry about that Mrs. Bullard, until we know. All any of us can do now is to give him the rest and care he needs. Nature is a wonderful healer, and God often moves in wondrous ways."

Dr. Matthews didn't need to tell us what would happen if the nerves were destroyed. All of us knew. Papa would never walk again! I couldn't bear to think of Papa as a helpless invalid the rest of his life. Surely, surely God would not be so cruel!

Shortly after Dr. Matthews left Elsie and Davey came. The sight of our tearful faces must have told her the doctor's verdict even before Mama put it into words. She cried very hard for a while, sobbing, "He did it to save Davey and you. He *has* to get well!"

Mama put her arms around her. "I know, darling. We will pray very hard that it is God's will. He is the Great Physician. We must all remember that." She brought Elsie a cup of coffee and held Davey close, humming the hymn she loved to herself—and perhaps to us too.

We lived though this day, and many to follow, in stunned anxiety. Neighbors came. The men to help with the farm work still to be done before winter set in, the women to bring prepared food and help with canning fruit and vegetables. Most of the time one of the women stayed the night to sit up with Papa while Mama rested. Dr. Matthews came every day. Except for the paralysis Papa seemed to be recovering rapidly. But none of us would soon forget his explosion the day Dr. Matthews told him how serious his injuries were.

"I *won't* be an invalid, Molly!" he yelled as soon as Dr. Matthews was out the back door. "That stupid doctor doesn't know what he's talking about. Let me up and I'll show him!" He pushed himself up struggling to make his legs obey. Finally, his face wet from the futile endeavor, he fell back exhausted. Then he clenched his jaws and tears of frustration filled his eyes. Suddenly he started cursing, loud blasphemous curses against God and doctors and horses. Even against Mama. He blamed her for dropping the reins.

Vina and I listened in horror. Mama made no effort to stop the terrible words that poured from his lips. She waited until he was calmer, then wiped the perspiration from his face and pulled the shades and led us from the room.

Outside, Vina and I cried, "Oh, Mama!" and clung to her.

"Shhh! Papa doesn't mean any of it. He's frightened. He wants to fight everybody, even God. It's a difficult thing he faces, girls. He needs our help and a lot of love and understanding. After a while he will know he needs God's help too."

It was a long time before Papa was willing to admit that.

After that one terrible outburst he lay quiet most of the time. He ate some of the food Mama brought him but refused to see anyone else except Dr. Matthews. Toward the end of that week he asked to see Uncle Ethan. Mama left them alone and drove to town. Uncle Ethan would stay until she returned. Now, more than ever, it was important the hardware business prosper and the buildings she owned remain rented. Soon Papa would be strong enough to make the trip to Sioux City. Whatever the verdict, it was going to take a lot of time and money to get Papa well again.

It was almost the end of September before Dr. Matthews agreed Papa was strong enough for the trip to Sioux City. He was still silent and depressed and would see no one except the Doctor, Uncle Ethan and Mama. He had flatly refused to see Rev. Pritchard who had come several times since his injury. Each time Rev. Pritchard had knelt with us in the quiet parlor and prayed for Papa's recovery. Surely, I thought, God would answer his prayers in spite of Papa's blasphemy.

The day Papa was to leave for Sioux City Dr. Matthews did not come out, but he had given Mama and Uncle Ethan instructions about preparing Papa for the trip, and he would meet them at the depot in town. Papa was moved onto a strong wide board covered with blankets, then strapped securely to it. Jed and Uncle Ethan carried him to the springwagon and Mama covered him with more blankets. Uncle Ethan would drive them to town and bring the springwagon back. Only Dr. Matthews and Mama would go with Papa to Sioux City.

We stood on the back porch and watched until the springwagon faded from sight, then went inside. Aunt Hilda insisted we eat some lunch before we went back to work. We ate, more to keep from thinking of the emptiness of the house than to satisfy an appetite.

Miss Engles returned from her vacation and came at once to see us. Mr. Evans was with her. He, too, had come several times since Papa's accident but Papa refused to see him. This was hard to understand. Papa and Mr. Evans always had seemed to be such good friends. Maybe he thought if he saw

Mr. Evans he'd have to see Rev. Pritchard, and the minister reminded him of his awful blasphemy. Or maybe Mr. Evans reminded him of all the things Papa thought he'd never be able to do again.

"Doctors do marvelous things these days," Miss Engles said when she had told us how sorry she was about the accident. "Your father is a rugged man, too. He'll fight hard to be well again. So you girls must not worry too much."

I wanted to serve them tea in the parlor but they insisted the kitchen was cozier, and coffee would be just fine. We talked mostly about school which would begin in late October this year. She said we were not to be disturbed if we had to start later than the others; she'd help us to make up the lost time. Mr. Evans told me, proudly, of the blue ribbon his entry at the Fair had won, and was surprised I hadn't known about the prize awarded to Mama for her plum butter. I doubted even Mama knew about it. That prize had been dearly bought. I wondered about the "why" of things. *If* there had been no Fair would Papa now be well and strong as he'd always been? Or was it really God's will that he must suffer and maybe never walk again?

Four days passed. Mama returned from Sioux City alone. Papa must remain in the hospital for at least two weeks. Dr. Matthews had stayed to learn about the treatments the specialist said Papa must have. If Papa responded to them satisfactorily he could then be brought home and the treatments continued under Dr. Matthews supervision. No one, it seemed, had been sure whether Papa would ever be able to walk again.

"But there is hope," Mama told us. "The nerves do not seem to be permanently damaged, the doctors said. With patience and care, and God's help, Papa has a good chance for complete recovery. But it will take time, maybe a long time. That is what we all have to face, girls. With courage and much prayer."

Suddenly Mama sat up very straight. She had that determined look on her face and her shoulders were squared, her head high. "Papa *is* going to walk again! He *must!* God will do His part. It's up to us to do ours. Let's not forget that for a single moment."

## CHAPTER X
## 1895-96

October brought light frost, then turned unseasonably warm. The countryside blazed with color. Sumac burned in fiery patches along roadsides. The orchard changed summer greens for rich browns, gold and scarlet. Yellow leaves from the cottonwoods floated down through quiet sunny days spreading a bright carpet. A soft blue haze hung on the horizon. Evenings many bonfires pricked the dusk and the air was filled with the fragance of woodsmoke and burning leaves. Against starry night skies the windbreak cast a dark pattern.

From the moment of Mama's firm declaration she seemed possessed with the "strength of ten." While we waited for further news about Papa she restored order and purpose to our lives. Once a week she went to town. Beef-butchering was still some weeks away. Surely by then we would know about Papa. The hospital had promised to telegraph Dr. Matthews if there were any unforeseen complications. No news must be considered good news.

There was a chill in the air as October lengthened. I wore a sweater and scarf when I brought the cows from pasture each evening. In the barren fields, some still scared from the fire, blackbirds gathered. High against the dusty skies long wedges of geese moved southward, and their cries seemed a sorrowful farewell. Surely, I thought, this was the most beautiful time of the year! And perhaps the saddest.

It was late afternoon when Mama returned from town that Saturday. She brought exciting news. Papa was responding to the treatments. If this continued for another week he could be brought home.

"This doesn't mean Papa is well enough to walk yet. He will need many more weeks of care perhaps before that is possible," she told us.

For the present it was enough that he would not die. And that there was happiness in Mama's eyes once more.

That night she wrote two letters. A long one to Grandma

telling her about the accident, and not to worry, Papa was going to be all right. A shorter letter went to Uncle Phil with the same news. She didn't read the letters to us before she sealed them, and there was a secret look in her eyes.

A week later Dr. Matthews brought the good news. Papa could come home. He explained that Papa was still "not out of the woods," and that the next few months were likely to be the hardest for Papa and for us. "A big, normally healthy man like Sam Bullard," he said, "is rarely an easy patient. Be patient with him and give him time. It may take more of that than we realize right now."

After supper Mama drove over to tell Elsie and Jed the good news. Soon the whole community knew Papa was coming home. One evening when we came from school, we found the dining-room had been converted into a temporary bedroom. Our lovely dining table and chairs were stored upstairs in their bedroom.

I did not go to school on Friday. I went to town with Mama and Aunt Hilda to bring back our supplies. Uncle Ethan followed in the springwagon. It would be left in town to bring Papa home. Dr. Matthews was waiting at the depot when we arrived.

"We should be back Sunday evening," Mama told me. "But if we're not you're not to worry. We may have to stay a day or two. Depends on Papa's strength. I want all of you to go to church on Sunday with Aunt Hilda, and say a special prayer for Papa. And tell Elsie to try to come over for dinner on Sunday. It will make Papa very happy if you're all there when he gets home."

Rev. Pritchard also said a special prayer for Papa on Sunday. The whole congregation joined in the "Amen." After church, when I shook hands with him and thanked him, he said, "God already has answered our prayers. Ann. Your father is able to come home. Please tell your mother I'll stop by later in the week. Perhaps he will feel like seeing me now that he is better."

Elsie and Jed and Davey came home with us after church. Will would take care of the chores that night. It was beginning to get dark when we heard the springwagon. Elsie and Jed went outside. I ran into the dining-room where the bed had been set up, and turned back the covers. Papa had his eyes closed when they carried him in. He groaned once when they

119

lifted him off the carrying-board, then lay quietly. Mama covered him and put her hand on his forehead for a moment, then tip-toed out.

"When he wakes up he will want to see all of you." She hugged us and asked if we were all right.

We gathered about the kitchen table to wait. Elsie poured coffee. Mama told us as much as she knew about Papa's condition. He would have to stay in bed for several more weeks, maybe months. But there was every reason to believe he would walk again. Even then it might be a long time before he could do any kind of heavy work. Maybe never.

"This is going to be a very difficult time for Papa. We must be patient even if he gets pretty grumpy at times."

Uncle Ethan got up. "I'd better be getting home. Hilda will be anxious for news of Sam."

Jed said he would take him in his buggy, and got his coat. Mama went to the door with them. "You know how grateful I am, Ethan, for everything. Please tell Hilda to come over as soon as she can. I think the sight of her will do Sam more good than almost anything else."

He laughed. "Wouldn't be surprised. The sight of her is sure going to do *me* a lot of good."

Supper was ready when Jed got back. It was good to be together again as a family, and to have Papa home. He was awake now. Mama fixed a tray and sat with him while he ate. Then we filed in, two at a time. Elsie and Davey first, then Lucy and Mae, and finally Vina and I. Mama cautioned us not to stay long. Papa was still pretty tired from the trip.

Seeing him there in the big bed, so helpless and thin and pale, it was hard to keep the tears back or to believe it was really Papa. He smiled at our long faces and hugged us. "Cheer up! I'm going to be out of this bed in no time. It's mighty good to be home."

"We got all the root crops in, Papa," Vina said.

"And the corn gathered and shucked," I added.

"Fine. Fine. I knew I could count on my girls."

Afterwards I thought he might have to depend upon us for a lot more for a long time. If he did, we wouldn't complain.

Jed went in then. He stayed longer than we had and we could hear them talking in low voices. "Don't worry about the farm work," Jed said. "Will and I will help. So will the neighbors. We want you well and strong again soon."

"Don't you worry about that, son. I'm going to be all right. You can't keep a good man down, you know!"

We went back to school on Monday. The routines of our lives resumed. Dr. Matthews came out that evening. He was with Papa quite a while. "Just you behave yourself, Sam. Don't go trying to rush things. Nature needs time. Let *me* be the judge of when you can try your legs."

He needn't have worried about Papa disobeying him. He seemed content to lie quietly, eat and sleep, saying very little after his first burst of confidence. This was so unlike Papa, even under the circumstances, I began to wonder if he secretly believed he would not walk again. Mama must have been worrying about that too.

"He's too quiet," she remarked one day when Papa had been home almost two weeks. We had finished the milking and were walking slowly back to the house with brimming pails. "It's not like Papa to be this moody. Something is bothering him. Honestly, child, I'd feel better if he yelled at us and complained."

I agreed with her but didn't say so. "Maybe he's only trying to do what Dr. Matthews says, Mama."

"Well, I hope that's all it is. But I do wish he'd see Rev. Pritchard. He wouldn't even let him into the room on Thursday when he stopped by."

"At least *that's* more like Papa. Being so stubborn."

Mama stopped and looked at me. "Yes. Maybe it *is* a good sign, Ann. I hadn't thought of it like that. But he shouldn't keep blaming God for what happened. He needs God's help more than ever now. We all do. He *has* to believe the doctors, and he *must* have faith. If only he'd talk to Rev. Pritchard he would see that. I've tried but I don't seem to have done very well."

I disagreed with that. "No one could have done more than you have, Mama. Please don't worry. Rev. Pritchard is a persistent man. He seems to find a way to do whatever needs to be done."

She smiled and looked relieved. "Yes, he does have a way with him, doesn't he. I'd forgotten that for a moment."

Walking on toward the house I remembered how much good

talking with him had done me. I'd had no chance to mention this to Mama. So much had happened since that afternoon at the Fair. I no longer thought of him as just a minister. He was also my friend. Someone I could talk to about the puzzles of life. And the older I became the more things seemed to puzzle me. The reasons for what happened or didn't happen. Grandma always said, "It's God's will." I didn't doubt that, but I couldn't help asking myself *why* it was God's will. Mama answered that with, "God moves in mysterious ways." I didn't doubt that either, but neither answer satisfied the questioning within me. I felt sure Rev. Pritchard would have the answers, *if* I ever had the chance to ask some of those questions. Not just Bible answers, but, well, *life* answers.

If Papa would listen Rev. Pritchard might be able to answer whatever was bothering him. And there was now no doubt something *was*.

Just before Thanksgiving the weather turned cold. All day and throughout the night the snow fell, blanketing the prairies and piling up deep drifts along the windbreak. Cy now did Papa's chores. He waded knee-deep drifts and drove us to and from school in the bobsled. On Saturdays he took Mama into town.

This year Thanksgiving dinner was especially festive. Our hearts were humble and overflowing with gratitude. Papa was at home, and whether he wanted to admit it or not, he was getting better. Uncle Ethan and Aunt Hilda, and Hans and Kathy, were our only guests, and they were really a part of the family. The big kitchen table was loaded with good things to eat. A golden brown turkey with apple stuffing sat in the middle of the table. The base-burner in the parlor glowed cherry-red, filling the whole house with warmth. Papa's bed was moved close to the open kitchen door so he could be a part of the family gathering even if he couldn't sit at the table. Aunt Hilda saw to it that everyone was in a good mood, including Papa. When she laughed, the rest of us couldn't help laughing too.

On Thursday, a week after Thanksgiving, Rev. Pritchard stopped by as he'd been doing every week, to inquire about Papa and talk with him if Papa would see him. He was later than usual today. I had just come in from school and was upstairs changing my dress. I could hear him talking with Mama in the kitchen below. Papa was asleep and Mama thought it best not to disturb him.

"You can take time for some coffee and doughnuts, can't you? The doughnuts are still hot, and so is the coffee."

"Indeed I can. I haven't been able to resist hot doughnuts since I was eight years old. That was the day I was allowed to have three, fresh from the frying pan."

"You may have *more* than three today, if you want them."

Rev. Pritchard sounded very cheerful considering he had come to call on a sick man. I had an idea he was trying to cheer Mama up a little.

"Two will be quite sufficient, thank you. How *is* Sam, Mrs. Bullard?

"Physically, he's much better. Spiritually, he's no better, I'm afraid. He's still blaming God for what happened to him. I do wish he'd talk with you, Rev. Pritchard."

"Give him time, Mrs. Bullard. Sam's reaction to the accident is a natural one. Most of us try to blame someone for things we don't understand. With Sam it's easier to blame God. *He* won't talk back or argue!"

"I see what you mean," Mama said, relief in her voice. "Sam does like to argue, although he's done less of it lately. Sometimes I think he's too quiet. It's not like him to want to be alone so much."

"It's not easy for a man as vital as Sam to have to be bedfast. Nor easy on you and the girls."

"I know. But the important thing is having him well again. I don't think he can be really well, Rev. Pritchard, so long as he hates God."

"Sam doesn't hate God. *You* must know that, Mrs. Bullard, even if he is trying to make himself believe it right now." He was silent a while. "I'd like to say something which may offend you for a moment, although it isn't intended to. Has it occurred to you that *your* staying away from church services may have something to do with Sam's attitude? Perhaps he feels that if attending church isn't important to you, God can't be very important to you."

"But I can't leave him alone."

"Why not?"

"He'd be terribly upset, and that would delay his recovery."

"I don't agree on either point. Sam is quite well enough to lie there and read a newspaper, or just sleep if he wants to, for a couple of hours. Oh, I know you can worship God right here, doing what you feel is your duty, Mrs. Bullard. But, personally, I don't believe God or Sam expects that of you. Your life must go on too. You need to see your friends, hear some music and, yes, even listen to one of my sermons, and, you haven't been to Literary Society either for more than two months."

Surprisingly, Mama laughed. "So! If you can't scold Sam, you can scold me. Is that it?"

"Surely, you must know I didn't mean . . ."

"Of course! The truth is, I needed a scolding. You're right. I'll be in your congregation next Sunday. I promise. This may be just the nudge Sam needs. Thank you, Rev. Pritchard."

"Why not start by coming to Literary Society tomorrow night?"

"I'd like to, but I think it would be best to wait until Sunday."

"Is there any reason why the girls shouldn't go? I'd be happy to come for them if they want to go."

"Well, I don't see any reason why Ann and Alvina shouldn't go. They *have* been pretty tied down lately. Are you sure it won't be inconvenient for you to take them? They could go with Ethan and Hilda."

"I'd be happy to call for them. Ethan's bob-sled would be pretty crowded with two more passengers." The kitchen chair creaked a little when he got up. "I'll come by about seven if that's all right. If Sam's in a better mood perhaps I can have a few words with him."

"Fine. The girls will be pleased to have a change. And thank you for giving me a new slant on things, Rev. Pritchard."

As soon as I was sure he was gone I went downstairs. "Why didn't you come down sooner?" she asked. "You're not avoiding Rev. Pritchard are you?

"Of course not. Why should I?"

"Well, we haven't been very regular church-goers lately. He's offered to take you and Vina to Literary Society tomorrow. Would you like that?"

"Aren't you going too?" I asked, pretending innocence of the offer.

"And leave Papa alone? But there's no reason why you girls can't go. He'll stop by about seven."

As things turned out, I went to Literary Society alone with Rev. Pritchard. Vina had a bad cold and Mama kept her in bed, wrapped in flannel with turpentine-and-grease on her chest.

The room was crowded when we arrived. Some of the girls gave us surprised, knowing looks, then began whispering among themselves. If Rev. Pritchard noticed he gave no indication of it. He took my coat and hung it up, and waited while I removed my hat, then escorted me to a seat. The program was about to begin. Nellie Hughes and Tom Simpson were seated across the aisle. She leaned to whisper something to him and smiled. I didn't mind for myself, but it wasn't exactly fair to Rev. Pritchard. It gave the wrong impression. I shouldn't have come without Vina. There would be talk. But as the evening progressed he didn't seem to mind in the least that there might be. When the literary program was over the seats were pushed back for dancing. Rev. Pritchard never joined in this, not even the square dances. I'd often wondered why. Did he think all dancing was sinful? Usually he would sit with one of the older members and talk while the dancing was in full swing.

Tonight when square dancing started, he said, "No reason for you to be a wall-flower because I must." And he insisted I join in. But when the waltzing began I sat beside Rev. Pritchard, watching. Mr. Evans and Miss Engles were among the first on the floor.

"Don't they dance beautifully together?" I commented.

"Yes," he admitted. "They're beautiful people. Beauty seems to flow from them as light from the sun."

I smiled. Again he sounded more like Mr. Evans than a minister. It was the kind of thing he would have said. I had not expected so much poetry from Rev. Pritchard. Then, suddenly Mr. Evans was standing before me.

"May I have the pleasure, Miss Ann?"

As I followed Mr. Evans' lead through exhilarating measures of a waltz, everything seemed suddenly right once more. He escorted me back to my seat and bowed. "That was delightful, my dear. I hope you will save at least one more for me."

125

I smiled and promised. As he hurried back to Miss Engles before someone else claimed her for the next dance, I looked up to find Bob Hughes standing before me, asking "the pleasure of the next dance." I felt a little guilty leaving Rev. Pritchard alone. After all, he had brought me.

But he quickly dispelled my concern. "Mrs. Phillips is waiting for me to help set up the refreshment table. Even the musicians are starting to look hungry!"

I had never danced with Bob Hughes before. He was a lot better dancer than I'd thought he might be. He seemed too big to be a good dancer. He was taller than Papa, and very muscular. That day at the Fair I'd seen him lifting weights I thought would break his back. But tonight he glided over the dance floor as easily as Mr. Evans had done. Maybe size had nothing to do with gracefulness on a dance floor; maybe it depended upon how he responded to the music, and how much gentleness there was inside him. It seemed too bad ministers weren't permitted to dance. They should be the best dancers of all!

Driving home later that evening through the crisp, cold, starlit night I was suddenly more than ever aware of Rev. Pritchard's gentleness. One expected gentleness and understanding from a minister, but tonight I sensed there was a difference; that this special gentleness was because he cared about me. And suddenly everything seemed new and different. The snow-wrapped world had never looked so beautiful, and there was a singing inside me.

When we reached home and he took my hand to help me down, he held it a while before he whispered good-night. Now I knew that tonight had been different for him, too.

As winter closed in with more snow and bitter winds, we adjusted to the new pattern of our lives. A pattern destined to have far greater significance than we knew at the time. Except Mama. Often she was late getting home from town on Saturdays and all evening she would be unusually thoughtful. I knew she was worried about Papa. Dr. Matthews said he should be able to sit up now a good part of the day, even demanding the right to try his legs. But Papa didn't want to sit up in a chair, and he acted like he didn't care whether he ever walked again. He read a little and slept a good deal. Since her talk with Rev. Pritchard Mama had included a Bible with other reading material left by Papa's bed. So far as we knew he had ignored the Bible. Until one evening shortly before Christmas. When Mama took his supper in to him she noticed the book-mark she had left in the Bible was lying on the table. It couldn't have fallen out unless he had opened the Bible.

"Even that would be a good sign," she told me. "If he's been *reading* it that's a very good sign."

It was, in one way. Perhaps Papa was beginning to realize he needed God's help to get well. But it might also mean he doubted he would ever walk without some kind of miracle. Papa always insisted "God helps them who help themselves, and I've been looking out for myself for a long time." He didn't examine the Bible quotation further. But Mama did. She would say, "That's true enough, Sam. But He *leads* us in the right path to help Him perform miracles. If we refuse to walk that path . . ." Usually by that time Papa had changed the subject. Maybe now he had been thinking about what "walking the path," really meant. He'd refused any help for a long time. Now perhaps he was ready to accept it.

Suddenly Christmas was upon us. With all the preparations I'm afraid most of us forgot about Papa's need for a miracle, at least for a while. Rev. Pritchard took me to a Christmas party at Mr. Evans' house. Vina was permitted to go with Gus, her first party with her own escort. Mama let her go only because the party was at Mr. Evan's place. Vina would be well chaperoned. But Papa had objected strenuously. I was in the parlor fixing the fire in the base-burner when Mama mentioned it to him.

"I'll swear I don't know what gets into you, Molly!" he shouted, sounding more like the Papa we knew. "Letting Vina drive off alone with Gus, or any boy. She's *only* fourteen, don't you realize that?"

"I do, Sam. And there's no need to shout and get all upset about it. Vina is a good girl and Gus is a fine boy, and they *are* going to a party at Mr. Evans' house, not to some public hall. Ann will be there and so will Ethan and Hilda."

"And that's another thing. How long has Ann been going out with Martin?"

"Oh, Sam! Ann hasn't been 'going out' with Rev. Pritchard, as you put it, at all. He's taken her to one Literary meeting, and he's taking her to this party on Tuesday. What's wrong with the girls going to these things even if we can't?"

"You can go if you want to. You don't have to stay here just because I'm flat on my back."

"I don't want to go without you, Sam. Don't you know that?"

Mama had kept her promise to Rev. Pritchard. She had taken us to church every Sunday since Thanksgiving. Papa insisted he didn't need anyone to stay with him, but Mama saw to it there was someone close by if he needed anything.

The night of the party Mama stayed at home with Papa. He had made a big fuss about it, told her she didn't have to be a martyr for him, and he didn't want anyone feeling sorry for him. Mama just smiled. I think she was happy he was well enough to shout and argue. When she told him she wasn't staying home just for his sake, that she was keeping Davey and Hans and Kathy so Elsie and Jed, Uncle Ethan and Aunt Hilda could have a good time, Papa settled down.


About the middle of February when she came back from town, Mama brought a letter for Papa from Uncle Phil. She took it to him right away as if she knew it was important, but she didn't stay to find out why.

"You can put the groceries away, Ann. I'll get supper started."

She was peeling potatoes when Papa called in a loud voice. "Molly! Come in here a minute."

Mama went quickly. I was glad she didn't close the door. From the sound of Papa's voice he was either excited or angry. I couldn't tell which. I moved closer to the door.

"Would you believe it? Phil wants to move to Iowa."

"Well, what's wrong with that?"

"Not a thing. But he sure didn't feel that way when we moved out here. He didn't come right out and say it then but I know he thought I was several kinds of a fool. *That's* what makes it so funny. Now he wants me to find him a piece of land close to Elmer. Doesn't he know there's not an acre of open land left in this whole area?" He stopped a second. "And I guess he doesn't know I'm flat on my back."

"You'll just have to tell him that, Sam. About the land and your accident."

Papa didn't say anything for a while. "What would you think about selling him this farm, Molly?"

"What would *you* think about it?"

"Well, I'm sure not going to be doing any farming for a while. Not that I intend to stay in this bed forever,"

Mama said softly, "You wouldn't *be* in that bed if I had held onto those reins, Sam. If you want to sell the farm to Phil it will be all right with me."

"I'm not blaming you for the accident. You know that. But spring plowing and planting have to be done and you and the kids can't do that alone."

"We could. With Cy and the neighbors to help."

"No, Molly. Cy's getting old and the neighbors have their own farm work to do. There's no telling how long it might be before I'm able to do what I used to do. Phil's son Fred must be full grown by now. They could handle this place, and they'd appreciate all we've built here."

"That's true. It wouldn't be like selling to a stranger. But are you sure you want to sell the farm, Sam?"

"Maybe. Let me think about it. Phil may not want to buy a ready-made farm. He only asked about land. But if he wants a real farm I just might decide to let him have this one."

Mama was smiling when she came back to the kitchen.

"Do you think Papa *will* sell Uncle Phil the farm?" I blurted.

"You were supposed to be putting the groceries away, young lady," she said sternly, but she was still smiling.

"I'm sorry, Mama. I couldn't help hearing . . . ."

"I know that, dear. We'll talk about it later." Vina and Lucy were coming in with the milk and eggs.

When supper was over and Papa was asleep, Mama sent Vina and Lucy and Mae up to bed. She asked me to stay, she had a lot to tell me. She closed the door to Papa's room and sat down beside me at the kitchen table. As she talked I understood more clearly what she had meant when she said, "God leads us in the right path to help Him perform miracles".

She told me that for some time she had known it was going to be necessary to sell the farm and move into town. For Papa's sake. Even when he was well again Dr. Matthews agreed farm work might be too much for him. Papa was beginning to realize that too. This didn't mean Papa would be an invalid the rest of his life. It only meant he would have to take things easier.

"But Papa can be pretty stubborn at times, as we all know. Even about things for his own good. Sometimes it's necessary to help him make up his mind without letting him know you've helped. This is one of those times, dear."

To do this, she had written Uncle Phil about Papa's accident and told him she felt it was best to sell the farm now and move into town; and wondered if Fred might be interested in buying it since Elmer and his family had the adoining farm; but if he wasn't interested she was sure Mr. Close would have no trouble finding a satisfactory buyer.

"He wrote me at once. He and Fred were interested, but he had to be sure he had a buyer for their farm before he wrote to Papa. Today Papa got that letter."

I thought about all she had said for a while. "If we *have* to sell the farm I'd sure like Uncle Phil to have it. But I'm surprised Papa is so willing to sell it to him. He's always been a little bit jealous of Uncle Phil."

"That was silly of him, of course. He's had a lot of time to think these past months. I'm sure he sees things differently now. But the farm means a lot to him. It's not going to be easy for him to sell it, to admit he can't handle it any more. I mustn't do any more meddling, Ann, and you're the only one besides Phil who knows I've done any. Let's keep it that way. And we'll let Papa make up his own mind about selling the farm."

I thought now of what Mama had said the day she bought the buildings and reopened the hardware store. That women in this new country had to be strong enough to do their own work and help men keep their "pioneering spirit". If selling the farm seemed like his idea, Papa would be able to accept it and keep his self-respect.

Papa didn't take long to make up his mind. The next night after supper he called for Mama, and to my surprise, asked me to come in too.

"Well, Molly, I've decided it might be best to sell Phil our farm. That is, if he wants it. But you and the girls should have something to say about it. We've all worked mighty hard to build up this place." He turned to me. "I suppose Mama has told you Uncle Phil wants to move out here, settle down nearer Elmer"

I admitted she had. "It would be nice having them here."

Mama said, "The children and I will do whatever you think best, Sam. We want you well again."

Papa was thoughtful for a while. "Then that settles it. Ann, bring me that tablet and pencil from the desk. I'll write Phil tonight. If he wants our farm and will pay what I ask, the place is his. He'll be getting the best danged farm in the County at any price. I hope he realizes that."

"Where are we going to live?" I asked, although I knew what Mama had in mind for us.

"Time enough to think about that after I hear from Phil." He propped himself up against the headboard and took the writing material. "Go on to bed, Ann. Mama and I have things to talk about."

Nothing more was said about where we would live until Uncle Phil's letter came a couple of weeks later. Mama was in with Papa quite a while. She waited until after supper to talk about it, and this time she asked Vina to stay.

"You're both old enough to know what is happening, but for the present let's keep all I'm going to tell you in the family." She told Vina about Uncle Phil's first letter. "Today Papa got Uncle Phil's reply to his offer. He is going to buy our farm. He and Fred will be here in a week or so, in time for spring plowing and planting."

Vina asked the same question I had. "Where are *we* going to live?"

"I'm coming to that. Today I spoke to Mr. Close about selling the grocery store building to Mr. Bruckner. He's been wanting to buy it for a long time and now has the money to buy. Also I found a house I can buy at a very good price. Papa says if Uncle Ethan thinks it's worth the price, it's all right with him. So tomorrow, after church, we'll drive in to town so he and you girls can see the place. I want you to be pleased with it too. If Jed can stay with Papa and the children, we'll take Aunt Hilda and Elsie with us."

"Didn't you talk to Mr. Plover about it, Mama?" I asked.

"Of course. But Papa isn't always ready to agree Mr. Plover has good judgment." She smiled.

Vina was probably thinking what I was. So often we had wished we could live in town. Now that it was about to happen we weren't sure we wanted to leave the farm. How could I bear to leave Mr. Evans and Miss Engles and Rev. Pritchard and all my friends at school? We'd be so far from Elsie and Jed and Davey and Uncle Ethan and Aunt Hilda we'd almost never see them.

Mama said, "I must say you don't look very pleased about all this."

"Oh, we are, Mama. Really we are, aren't we Vina?" She nodded. "It's just that...."

".... you don't like leaving all your friends here. Is that it? It's only a few miles to town, girls. We can come out as often as you like to see Elsie and Davey and Jed and the others."

I felt ashamed to have put my wishes ahead of everyone else. "If it's best for Papa and you we'll like living in town. Won't we Vina?"

This time she agreed with enthusiasm. "No more wading snowdrifts or mud to get to school! No more barnyard chores to do!"

"Oh, don't be so sure about all that, young lady!" Mama laughed. "It snows in town, and the streets do get muddy, and the house I expect to buy does have a barn."

"Just the same, I'm going to like living in town. Honest, Mama."

She got up and closed the door into Papa's room. "Fine, girls. Now I have more news which I haven't told Papa as yet. I got a letter from Grandma today. She's worried about Papa and the extra work it means for all of us. Besides, I'm sure it gets pretty lonely being so far away from us. Anyway, she has decided to come out and spend the summer."

We were so excited it was hard to keep our voices down. "When, Mama? When will she be here?"

"As soon as she closes up her house, I suppose. She'll let me know. Of course she doesn't know we're selling the farm. Unless Uncle Phil has told her and I don't think he would without asking me first. I'll write her about all of it as soon as we have decided on the house."

"How big is it?" Vina wanted to know.

"Big enough. But you'll see for yourselves tomorrow. Now

you better get to bed. We've got a big day ahead of us tomorrow." She got up and poured a glass of milk and cut a wedge of chocolate cake for Papa's night-snack. "And girls, we won't talk about the new house to anyone at church tomorrow, remember."

"Of course we won't."

But that promise didn't apply to ourselves. Vina and I lay awake a long time talking about the exciting things that were happening. She was as reluctant to leave her special friends as I was. Many things we had looked upon as chores, suddenly became privileges which we would have no more. Driving the cows to pasture and bringing them in at nightfall when the whole world was a place of pink and gold; roaming the fields in springtime seeing who could find the most early flowers; and bobsled rides across snowy fields to Literary Society.

"What *will* we do in town?" Vina finally asked.

When we saw the house Mama had selected all our doubts vanished. It was such a big house! Two stories high, painted white with blue trimmings around windows and doors. Across the front and around one side was a wide porch with a balustrade, and there was a picket fence around the front yard. A big cottonwood shaded the front porch. At one side were two lilac trees. The trees were barren now but it was not hard to imagine how they would be in spring and summer. The small porch at the back was screened, with bushes on each side of the steps and along the walk that led to a barn. Mama said it was a "carriage house"; that the barn was farther back.

Inside, the house seemed to us a palace. There was a wide entrance hall which led into a big living room with a fireplace. On each side of it were bookcases with stained-glass windows above them. Glass doors separated the living-room from the dining-room. Beyond, through a swinging door, was the kitchen with many cupboards and a pantry.

We ran back to the front hall and started up the stairway. Mama called to us. "Let's explore the downstairs first girls."

Now we saw that there were two more rooms across the entrance hall. "This one will be the parlor and library," she said proudly. "The other will be a bedroom for Papa until he is able to climb the stairs."

Vina asked, "May we see the upstairs now?"

Mama led the way. Here was a wide hallway too. Off it were four bedrooms. At the far end, over the back porch, was a smaller bedroom with gabled roof and windows which opened outward, like pictures I had seen of English houses. And, wonder-of-wonders, there was a bathroom complete with tub and water closet! No more wading snowdrifts to get to the privy. No more taking turns in the kitchen on Saturday night to bathe in Mama's biggest washtub.

It was all too grand to believe. Mama just *had* to buy this house!

Uncle Ethan had done his own exploring. He agreed the house was in good condition and well worth the price the Stebbins Estate was asking for it. Now we understood why the house was so grand. He said one of the Stebbins boys had built it for his Eastern bride. She was so unhappy in this wild new country he had been forced to take her back to Philadelphia. They had lived in the house, Mr. Close said, scarcely six months. It had been empty ever since, more than a year now. Few families who needed so much space could afford to buy it.

Dear Grandpa! If he hadn't left Mama all that money we couldn't have afforded it either. And now Grandma would be here this summer to share it with us.

Vina sighed as we went slowly down the stairs. "Honestly, Ann, sometimes life is just *too* wonderful."

# CHAPTER XI
## 1896

March came in "like a lamb". Chinook winds cleared most of the snow from the prairies. Only a few patches remained around the barn and shaded places along the windbreak. The weather was balmy with an unmistakable smell of spring. Little green clumps began to appear in meadows and pastures. Evenings I watched thin black lines of wild geese against an opal sky, winging northward. A sure sign winter was past.

The first week in March Uncle Phil and Fred arrived. Uncle Phil's hair was greyer and thinner on top, otherwise he hadn't changed very much. Fred, who had been just a skinny boy of thirteen when we left Saunemin, now was almost as big as Elmer. He was good looking too. As he shook hands with me I thought he was in for quite a chase. There were still several unmarried girls in the community!

Papa was in high spirits. "Well, Phil, you old son-of-a-gun!" he greeted. "Finally got smart, eh, and decided to come to the good land?"

"I don't know how smart I am, but I'm here," he laughed. "How are you, Sam? It's sure mighty good to see you."

"I'm doing all right. And let me tell you! You'd have been a lot smarter if you'd come out here when I did."

"Oh, I don't know about that! Maybe I was waiting for you to get the country opened up. Seriously, Sam, you've done a fine job, you and Molly and the girls."

"You're danged right we have. And if it weren't for these useless legs of mine I wouldn't sell it at any price."

"I know, Sam. I'm mighty sorry about that. But let's get one thing straight right now. When you're up and around again if you want to buy the farm back I'll sell it to you for exactly what I'm paying you for it. You have my word on that."

Papa's face was suddenly grave. "That might be quite a while, Phil. But thanks anyway."

Mama had supper ready, a real feast. After the dishes were washed we girls gathered around Fred in the parlor. We had a hundred questions to ask about our old farm and the people we knew there, and he was eager to hear about life in Iowa. Mama and Uncle Phil remained in Papa's room, talking. I could hear parts of their conversation.

"It's hard work, Phil. Make no mistake about that," Papa declared. "But this rich Iowa soil pays a man well for his labors. In another week the ground will be ready for the plow. Molly and the kids should have the packing done by then so we can clear out and leave the place to you and Fred. Did Molly tell you about our new house?"

"She sure did. Sounds mighty grand to me. If I weren't still a hard-bitten old farmer, I'd envy you all that ease and luxury."

"It won't be all ease and luxury. We've got the hardware store and some real estate in town to look after."

"Yes, Molly told me about that too."

I wondered just how *much* Mama had told him. Presently Elmer arrived to get Uncle Phil and Fred. They would stay at his place until we moved into town.

As it turned out, we didn't move until May. Mama wanted us to complete the school term. I was to be graduated this year and she thought I shouldn't change schools now. Uncle Phil said he and Fred ought to stay at Elmer's place anyway until the crops were in. When his furniture arrived he would have it stored in town until we were ready to move. Mama thanked him. Papa wasn't so understanding. At least not when he talked with Mama.

"School's not all that important,Molly. If we're going to move let's get it over with. What difference does it make where Ann graduates? Or *if* she graduates? First thing we know she'll be getting married anyway. Then what's the good of all that education?"

"It will make her a better wife and mother."

"In a pig's eye! If a girl knows how to cook and sew and bear healthy children, that's education enough."

"Perhaps. If that is all the education *she* wants. Ann wants more learning than most girls do and she has the capacity for it."

"Well, be that as it may, I've sold this farm to Phil. He has a right to what he bought and the comfort of his own house."

"Phil's in no big hurry. He likes being with Elmer, Nora and little Bobbie. And aren't you forgetting, Sam, that once we get moved you won't be able to see Davey quite so often? Besides, you'll be stronger by the time school's out."

"Then why in thunder did you let me sell the farm in the first place?"

"Because I was thinking of you. We all want you well again, and on your feet." Papa calmed down. He had no more objections.

Mama came back to the kitchen where I was setting the table. I asked her if waiting until I graduated before we moved was going to delay Papa's recovery.

"On the contrary. He needs more time to be strong enough for the move."

Maybe it was selfish but I couldn't help being glad we weren't going to move right away. I wanted my graduation to be with Miss Engles. And I liked Rev. Pritchard very much. If we moved to town before Papa made up with him, he probably never would. Papa was well enough to argue and shout sometimes, but he still refused to talk to Rev. Pritchard. "What I don't need, Molly, is a sermon," he said whenever Mama mentioned that Rev. Pritchard had called.

Martin (as he now insisted I call him) had taken me to Literary meetings several times since last November. My feelings toward him were much deeper than friendship but I wasn't sure I was in love with him. And I wasn't at all sure how he felt about me. Oh, I knew he liked me and enjoyed talking with me, but Mr. Evans felt that way toward me too and I knew he wasn't in love with me. He was in love with Miss Engles.

With Uncle Phil's and Fred's arrival the news soon got around that Papa had sold our farm and bought a house in town. For a while this was the principal topic of conversation wherever we went—at school, church and Literary Society. The rumors about Rev. Pritchard and myself were forgotten for a while at least. Or so I thought.

Mrs. McCavity cornered me at Literary meeting. "I hear you're going to be moving into town, Ann. Is it true your father has bought that big Stebbins house?"

I told her it was. "But we won't be moving until school is out."

She went on as if she hadn't heard me. "He *must* have received a *very* good price for the farm to be able to afford *that* house." Mrs. McCavity always talked in superlatives.

"I wouldn't know about that. But I'm sure Mama would be pleased to have you stop by for tea when you come to town."

"I'd love to. Do *thank* your mother for me. We're going to *miss* all of you *so* much." She leaned closer to whisper, "And I imagine a certain party is going to miss you *very much* indeed!"

The musicians, tuning up for square dancing, saved me from having to answer.

Driving home from Literary meetings was always the best time for Martin and me. We could relax and be ourselves without worrying about what someone was going to make out of a smile or a gesture. And we could talk about things that interested us, not what we were expected to say. I knew now Martin not only seemed different from other ministers I had known, he was different. One particular conversation had made me fully aware of this. We had been discussing a critical comment Mrs. Wiley had overheard and felt it her duty to report to "the Reverend".

"Serving God doesn't mean shutting yourself away from life," he said. "On the contrary. To truly serve God and minister to His people one must understand all phases of life. Without that understanding how can he make others who need help and guidance see that to *live* God's way is the fullest expression of life and of the human soul?"

"I think I know what you mean. You want people to do the right thing from choice, not because they fear the fires of hell."

"Exactly. You see, Ann, I could never accept the concept of God which was taught to me as a child, and even in church when I was older. *The Lord thy God is a jealous God. An eye for an eye* . . . . Not literally anyway. The God I believed in and still do, is a loving God. He does not want us to suffer. He gave us spiritual laws by which to live so that we need *not* suffer. If we break those laws it is not God who punishes us. We bring punishment upon ourselves."

I sighed. "You make it sound so simple."

"In a way it is. But doing right is not always easy, especially if we have selfish motives and think they might be better served by ignoring right."

"So *we* have to make a choice?"

"God gave us the right of choice. In all things. He never *forces* us to follow Him, walk His way."

I thought about that for a few minutes. Martin had never tried to force Papa to see him or listen to him, but he must have known he could help him if he could talk with him. Still, he was waiting for Papa to make the choice.

"You understand so much," I said. "No wonder you're different from other preachers. You're a *minister*, not just a preacher."

"Is there a difference?" he teased.

"I'm serious, Martin. I believe there is an important difference. I think I never understood what it was until tonight, listening to you. A preacher, it seems to me, reads and speaks the Word of God. A minister understands His Word and lives by it and teaches others how to follow Him. He truly ministers to those who need help and guidance."

He was silent for a while. "You're a remarkable young woman, Ann Bullard," he finally said. The tone was bantering but I knew he was serious. "You think things through, don't you?"

"I try to. Things must make sense to me before I can really believe. Is that wrong?"

"Certainly not. However, a label, or a title, is not always important. Perhaps it never is in the true sense of the word. If a man is truly a man of God in his heart, whether he is called preacher or minister or doctor makes little difference."

"But you're *good*, Martin, without being so solemn you frighten away those who need your help. They can talk with you, and you understand."

"I hope so. I don't know how 'good' I am Ann, but one thing I am sure of. I want to serve God to the best of my ability, and in the way He wants me to serve Him. That is often the most difficult problem we have to face. Knowing *how* He wants us to serve. I went through a terrifying period of self-doubt at the Seminary. Most students were solemn and seldom smiled about anything. So were our instructors. I concluded this was the proper conduct for a minister. But I couldn't *feel* solemn and long-faced. Serious, yes. The ministry is a serious undertaking. But to me it was also a joyous undertaking. I wanted to shout His wondrous truths from my pulpit, even from mountaintops. I *couldn't* believe God wanted me to go about with a long face as though serving Him made me miserable."

I laughed. "I can't imagine *you* with a long face! But a lot of folks doubted you were a fit minister when you first came because you weren't solemn."

"Did they really? Why didn't you tell me this before?"

"Oh, we changed our minds after your first sermon. Even Papa. He said you might be young but you sure could preach!"

We laughed together. As we often did about many things. It was as if the joy of being alive bubbled up inside us and spilled over. We rarely discussed the ministry. Mostly we talked about books and music and places he had visited. He seemed to know almost as much about books as Mr. Evans. I think he knew more about music. Often he told me about concerts and operas he had attended in Philadelphia and New York, and described them so vividly I could imagine I was there with him. I had always loved music. Now I yearned to hear great music, and see the places where great orchestras performed.

Once we discussed dancing. I told him I wondered why so many older people in our community thought it sinful, and I asked why he never danced even the square dances. "Do you think it's wrong to dance?" I asked bluntly.

"That depends upon the individual I believe. Even right things can be made evil if you have wrong intentions. Dancing *should* be an expression of joy. It began as that. The mass rejoicing of happy people. And to many people it still is. No one could doubt that watching Hilda Stone dance!" I agreed with that. "But there are also those who think anything which gives pleasure is wrong. That to be good you must be unhappy. They see ugliness and sin in dancing because *their* thoughts are ugly and sinful."

"Did you go to dances before you decided to become a minister?"

"Of course. Most young people in our community danced when they were happy, or to celebrate some special event. But the truth is I didn't really *learn* to dance until I went to the seminary."

"Did they *allow* you to dance there?"

140

He laughed. "Oh, no, indeed. But about the time I entered the seminary, I decided knowing how to dance properly was part of my education. Not that I expected to have much time for dancing once I was ordained. But it seemed important to understand what it might mean to my parishoners. So I found a teacher, a charming mature woman who made a modest living teaching people like myself who hadn't had the time or the opportunity to learn properly. For a couple of months I had a lesson every week. I didn't mention this to anyone at the seminary but somehow they found out about it. I thought I'd be asked to leave, give up my studies. Fortunately the Dean was more understanding than most of my professors. He accepted my explanation, and believed me when I told him I had not intentionally kept those studies secret, which was certainly the truth. But I had to give up the lessons."

"Is that the reason you don't dance now?"

"In a sense. You see, personally I see nothing wrong about dancing. But I try not to force my beliefs upon others. Many in this community would be greatly offended if I joined in the square dancing, and they'd be outraged if I waltzed half a measure. This might drive them away from church on Sunday and I'd have no chance to reach them with God's Word. Giving up dancing is a small sacrifice to that greater cause, wouldn't you agree?"

I was thinking of that particular discussion as we drove away from the school house. I had so much wanted to dance with him tonight. Why did the church permit such a rule? Perhaps, as Martin had said, they expected ministers to set an example. But if it were wrong for a minister to dance even a square dance shouldn't the church forbid it for everyone? It just didn't make sense.

I looked up at the starlit sky. The night was too beautiful to fill it with useless inner arguments. The freshness of spring was in the air. Martin sat beside me in his fine new buggy which the community had given him last Christmas. The mare was a gift from Mr. Evans. Its hooves, clipping along over the hard-packed road, seemed to emphasize the sadness in my heart. Soon we would be moving away. I would see him less and less. And maybe not at all unless Papa stopped blaming God, and Martin indirectly, for his accident.

His question echoed my thoughts. "When will you be moving to town, Ann?"

"Oh, not for a while. Not until school is out."

"That's not very long. I understand school will close earlier this year because of the early spring."

"I hadn't heard that. Is it definite?"

"So far as I know. Ben said about May first."

"That *isn't* very far away, is it? Mama still has to make my graduation dress. And I've a lot more studying to do before those final exams."

"And after graduation, what then?"·

"I don't know yet. Mama wants me to go to an Eastern school—Philadelphia or Boston. Papa thinks education for a girl is a waste of time and money. Especially, he says, 'in those fancy schools!' Miss Engles thinks I'd like the Academy in St. Louis where she went. *She* is a mighty good recommendation for it, don't you agree?"

He laughed. "You won't get an argument from me on that."

I sighed. "But all those places are so far away. Why isn't there a good school nearer to Stebbinsville?"

"Not enough need for it, I suppose. Many young ladies want only to learn reading and writing and arithmetic, and some scarcely bother with that much study."

"But there is so *much* to learn, Martin. So many things I want to know more about. Music, really great music. And art. Not just pretty pictures to hang on a farm-house wall, but the fine paintings found in museums and maybe in fine homes. Miss Engles says I could be a writer if I wanted to, but I'm not sure about that. I love books, but writing them . . . well, that takes a special talent, doesn't it?"

He pulled gently on the lines. The mare eased to a stop, and he took my hands. "With your enthusiasm, my dear, I've no doubt you can do anything you set your mind to. You will always soak up learning as a sponge absorbs water." He sighed. "And I'm going to miss you *very* much. Even Stebbinsville's too far away to suit me!"

I wanted to tell him I felt the same way, that any place without him was too far away, but that would seem bold and unladylike.

"Thank you, Martin." I said. "It's not going to be easy to leave here."

"You will permit me to see you in town, won't you?"

"I'd like that very much. I'm *not* so sure about Papa!"

We both laughed. Suddenly what Papa thought or did wasn't very important. Just being with Martin was all that mattered.

Grandma wrote she would come the end of April. She simply couldn't wait any longer, she said, to see all of us. And she hoped the bad weather was over. Besides, she added, she wanted to see me graduate, and Mama needed her to help with the moving. Dear Grandma! She always had to have a reason for what she did.

Mama read only part of Grandma's letter to Papa. "I know how much you and Sam and the children have put into that farm, Molly, and I'm sorry you had to sell it. But your new house sounds fine. It will be better for all of you living in town, including Sam. The children are growing up and need advantages the farm can't give them."

Papa didn't say very much but he seemed glad Grandma was coming for the summer. In fact he was happier about most things since Uncle Phil bought the farm. I think he must have worried more than we knew about us and the farm and whether he would ever walk again. Now all these worries were over. Even he no longer doubted that he would soon be able to walk. Dr. Matthews insisted that he sit up in the Morris chair a couple of hours each day at least. Getting in and out of bed was still painful. Pretty soon, the doctor said, he could manage a wheel chair.

That brought an explosion. "You're not getting *me* into a contraption like that! Not on your life!"

"It's your life I'm thinking about," Dr. Matthews said calmly.

"Well, you can *stop* thinking about it! I walk on my own two legs or I won't walk at all."

"We'll talk about that when the time comes." He took his hat and coat and left.

Having no one to argue with, Papa quieted down. Mama and I were in the kitchen. She looked at me and smiled. "Papa's certainly a lot better today."

I nodded and went on peeling potatoes for supper.

On Sunday, about the middle of April, Rev. Pritchard had a surprise for us.

"It is my pleasure to announce the engagement of Miss Julia Engles to Mr. James Evans." The congregation's whispered "Ah" interrupted him. "The wedding will take place here two weeks from today after our regular church services. There will be a reception for the young couple at the parsonage. You are all cordially invited."

It was after one o'clock when we got home and Mama gave Papa the news.

"Well, I guess it's no surprise to most folks," he said. "Jim's been sweet on her from the minute he saw her. Anyone could see that. He's getting a mighty fine wife, and Julia's not doing so bad either, if you ask me! They don't come any finer than Jim Evans. When did you say the wedding is, Molly?"

"Two weeks from today, after church."

"Your mother should be here by then, shouldn't she?"

"I hope so. She'll send a telegram about the exact day."

"Well, whether she's here or not, you're all going to that wedding. It's not going to kill me to stay here a few hours by myself. Besides, I'm getting tired of being treated like an invalid."

Mama smiled and told Vina and Lucy to go upstairs and change their dresses. "Dinner will be ready in a minute."

"Why can't we change them after dinner?" Vina asked. "I'm hungry, and besides, I like feeling dressed up for Sunday dinner."

"Put on your chambray, both of you. They're pretty enough for Sunday and easier washed."

The next two weeks were busy ones. Mama had my graduation dress almost finished. It was white voile with a lace yoke, and lace set into the skirt. It was long, almost touching the floor. I thought it the most beautiful dress any girl ever had. Vina worried about what to wear to the wedding.

"Why all the fuss?" I teased. "*You* aren't getting married."

"Well, I just *might* catch the bridal bouquet! If I do I want to look pretty."

"You'll look pretty anyway," Mama told her.

She thought about that for a minute. "*Am* I pretty, Mama? Gus says I am but I think he's teasing me."

"Yes, dear. You're a very pretty girl. But don't spoil it with vanity. Remember what Grandma says. 'Pretty is as pretty does.' And she's right."

On Tuesday the telegram from Grandma arrived. She would be on the Thursday afternoon train. Just in time for my graduation and the wedding. It seemed like everything was happening at once. And all of them happy things.

Vina and I were excused from school on Thursday afternoon and went with Mama to meet the train. Except for her completely white hair Grandma didn't look a bit older than when we last saw her. She hugged us and exclaimed over how much we had grown and how glad she was to see us. Then she asked about Papa.

"He's getting along fine," Mama told her. "Selling the farm and moving to town seems just the medicine he needed."

"When will you be moving?"

"Next week I imagine. Ann's graduation is tomorrow evening. And on Sunday our schoolteacher, Miss Engles, is being married to one of our finest citizens, Jim Evans. Big doing for our little community!"

"Looks like I got here just in time," Grandma laughed.

After supper that night, when Elsie, Jed and Davey had gone home, we talked about my graduation. Mama agreed to let me wear my hair up. "It will look better with your long dress," she said.

Papa insisted everyone must go to the graduation exercises. "I'll be all right by myself. It's a big day for Ann."

His remark surprised me. For someone who thought education was wasted on girls, he was being mighty considerate. Maybe he *was* proud of me. Why couldn't he tell me so? It would have been the nicest graduation present I could have.

Graduation exercises were set for seven o'clock on Friday evening. This would be the largest graduation class since Goldenrod school opened. Six of us. Hattie Simpson, Bob Hughes, Will Miller, Nettie Jenkins and Donna Elsworth, a newcomer to the community. Two rows of chairs were set up for the graduates at the left of the speaker's table, facing the audience. The boys sat in the back row, the girls in front. Nora Phillips opened the ceremony with the National Anthem in which everyone joined. Rev. Pritchard gave the invocation. He commended our futures to "God's guidance into paths of righteousness and service to Him," as we crossed this threshold into young manhood and womanhood. He beseeched us to "remember the days of our youth", and what we had learned here so that our days might be "long and fruitful in this wonderful land God had given us".

Nellie Hughes sang *Melody in F.* "Welcome, bright springtime, what joy now is ours . . ." The words, so appropriate to this special day, seemed to float from her throat filling the day with true rejoicing.

Mr. Evans, introduced by Mr. Hughes, now stood before us to deliver the Commencement address. I listened with only part of my mind. Mostly I was thinking of the influence he had had on my life. Because of him I had read more than most young people ever read, especially in rural areas. He had taught me to appreciate books not only as a source of learning and pleasure but as a guide to new experiences and clearer thinking. Listening to him now my heart swelled with gratitude.

Afterwards diplomas were awarded as each of us stepped forward to receive what we had worked so hard to earn. Then, in final tribute, Miss Engles addressed us briefly. She spoke directly to us, her back to the audience. She told us how proud she was of us and expressed the hope that we would find life richer and more rewarding because of these years together in Goldenrod schoolhouse. Rev. Pritchard spoke the benediction. Family and friends pressed about to extend congratulations before the refreshment table claimed their attention.

On my way to join Mama and Grandma, Mr. Evans stopped me. "Could you spare me a moment or two, Ann?"

"More than that, if you wish," I said, puzzled.

He drew me aside, away from the crowd. "You're lovely, my dear, in your grown up dress. I wanted to tell you how very proud of you I am. Julia tells me your grades were remarkably high in every subject. That's a fine record, Ann, something to be proud of the rest of your life."

"Thank you. So much of it I owe to you. You gave me those books that were beyond me, books to stretch my mind you said. And they *did* make me think beyond my environment, Mr. Evans. I can say thank-you now with more meaning. I'm very grateful to you."

He smiled. "You make me very proud, Ann. What will you do now?"

It was almost the same question Martin had asked. I gave him the same answer.

"Your mother is right, of course. You must go on to school. It would be a tragedy not to give your fertile mind a chance, whether that chance comes in Philadelphia or Boston or St. Louis." He smiled. "But you have the whole summer in which to decide. Let's go have a big piece of your mother's coconut cake."

I scarcely saw Martin after the benediction. The family and friends of other graduates kept him busy. But he drove me home.

There was a special quiet beauty to this spring night. A peacefulness after the excitement of the past week. He drove slowly, and for a while we did not talk. I knew that I was in love with him, and I understood what Mama had meant when she said there were several kinds of love. This was different from the way I had cared for Mr. Evans. This was a quiet certainty that I wanted to be with him the rest of my life. Suddenly the time seemed very short. The summer would pass quickly and I'd go away to school in some far-away place and maybe lose him forever. Oh, I just couldn't let that happen!

The excitement of graduation and my anxiety about the future were soon forgotten in the preparation for Miss Engles' wedding. Rev. Pritchard asked me to help Nellie and Donna with the decorations. We spent most of Saturday gathering spring flowers and green branches, and trying out different arrangements. When we were through we all agreed it looked just right. The altar was banked with white daisies on a bed of bright green leaves. Huge pots of pink apple blossoms stood on each side of the pulpit and at the back of the rostrum. For the parsonage, where the reception would be held, we gathered big bunches of yellow and purple crocus, yellow and white daisies and deep pink plum blossoms.

When the flower arrangements were in place the other girls went home. I stayed to help Mrs. Wiley and Mrs. Hughes arrange the table. Aunt Hilda was making the wedding cake. Other foods would be brought by various members of the congregation on Sunday morning.

"I doubt much attention will be paid to your sermon to-morrow," I told Martin on the way home.

"I've been thinking the same thing. So I've prepared a very short sermon. One I trust will set the right spiritual tone for the ceremony." He didn't even hint at the text and I didn't ask, but I was curious.

Sunday was a perfect spring day. Even Nature, I thought, is smiling on this wedding. Aunt Hilda was at the parsonage ahead of us. The big white wedding cake sat at one end of the long table which now gleamed with silver and fine china lent for the occasion. Mama's coffee service, which had been *her* wedding present, sat beside the cake. Mrs. Hughes came in carrying a large box which I learned contained Miss Engles' wedding dress sent from St. Louis. She put it in the bedroom away from the curious, and would help Miss Engles change into it after church.

Martin preached to a capacity congregation that morning. They appeared to be attentive despite the forthcoming event.

"This morning I shall read to you from the *Song of Solomon*, second chapter." He paused, then read in measured tones:

> My beloved spake and said unto me, 'Rise up, my love, my fair one, and come away.
> For lo, the winter is past, the rain is over and gone;
> The flowers appear on the earth; the time of the singing of birds is come, and the voice of the turtle is heard in our land;
> The fig tree putteth forth her green figs, and the vines with the tender grape give a good smell.
> Arise, my love, my fair one, and come away.'

He closed the Bible. The congregation became very still. He spoke briefly, his voice low, of the deeper meaning in Solomon's song: The power and majesty of God's eternal love for mankind made manifest in the flowering land and the singing of birds. And man's love for God and the world He had created for man's home, filling it with living, growing beauty, renewed each springtime in glorious promise. And, finally, of the wondrous love of a man for a woman.

Listening to these beautiful and solemn words I felt he was

148

speaking only to me, telling me of *his* love. But as I glanced about me I knew everyone in the congregation this morning had found some personal meaning in Martin's sermon.

The wedding ceremony was set for one o'clock. This left an hour after church for Miss Engles and Mr. Evans to change. And time for the rest of us to have coffee which Mrs. Wiley and Mrs. Jenkins served on the parsonage porch. The feasting would come after the wedding. We were back in our seats before one o'clock awaiting the big event.

Nora Phillips broke the tense silence with the opening strains of Mendelssohn's Wedding March. All heads turned toward the entrance, eager for a first glimpse of the bride.

Escorted by Mr. Hughes, Miss Engles moved in measured steps down the long aisle. As regal as a princess! Her gown was of creamy satin with a bodice covered by tiny pearls. The full flowing skirt touched the floor in front, extending into a modest train at the back. Her wedding veil, edged in tiny pearls, matched the color of her gown and rippled softly about her face and shoulders. Her hair shone like a bright crown. She carried a bouquet of pale yellow crocus laced with white daisies and soft ferns.

Mr. Evans joined her at the altar. The ceremony began.

It was the first wedding I had ever attended. I understood now why people wept at weddings. It was so solemn and awesome and beautiful. The tears in my eyes were happy ones for two wonderful people I loved very much.

"I now pronounce you man and wife," Rev. Pritchard intoned.

Mr. Evans kissed his lovely bride. Then arm in arm they walked slowly up the aisle to the vestibule and turned, their faces radiant. Instantly the solemn quiet was shattered. Friends and neighbors crowded around with congratulations. The women exclaimed over Julia's magnificent gown and what a *beautiful* bride she was. The men clamored to kiss the bride.

When she could make herself heard, Julia announced, "Hilda has baked us a beautiful wedding cake. Let's see if it is as good as it looks!"

The crowd followed to the parsonage and gathered around the table while she cut the cake. She insisted Rev. Pritchard must have the first piece.

"Does that mean you're next, Rev. Pritchard?" Mrs. Mc-

Cavity asked, laughing, and looked straight at me. I felt my face getting red, but waited for what Martin would say to her.

"Julia knows I'm the best judge of cake in the whole County, Mrs. McCavity," he said easily. *"She's* much too excited today to judge a cake." He took a big bite, savoring it solemnly. "Perfect! Worthy, indeed, of the occasion *and* Hilda Stone's culinary magic!"

Everyone laughed. Ben Miller quipped, "You didn't expect him to tell you, did you, Mrs. McCavity?" She accepted the ribbing in good humor. And a big piece of wedding cake. Later, as she brushed past me she smiled knowingly.

Now the feasting began. Huge platters of sliced ham and chicken and roast beef, several bowls of potato salad, pickles, and stacks of bread-and-butter sandwiches. Mrs. Jenkins and Aunt Hilda filled the plates as the guests filed past. Mama proudly dispensed coffee with sugar and cream. Both hands filled, the crowd soon spilled out onto the porch utilizing the other table.

I sat with Nellie and Hattie, and Donna the newcomer to the community. We balanced heaped plates on our knees and talked about the bride. "Did you *ever* in your life see *anything* as beautiful as Miss Engles . . . I mean Mrs. Evans' dress?" Hattie exclaimed breathlessly.

"Not a dress, silly! A *gown,"* Donna corrected. "And I bet it cost a fortune. Did you see all those *pearls* on the bodice and veil?"

"Now who's silly?" Hattie countered. "They're not *real* pearls."

Donna was not one to let her opinion be ridiculed. "Don't you think I *know* that? I also know *any* kind of pearls cost a lot. And so *many* of them!"

Nellie changed the subject. "Where do you think they'll go for their honeymoon?" She giggled meaningfully.

"No one knows *that!"* Donna said. "But you can bet it *won't* be the Stebbins House." Everyone laughed.

I listened, thinking how silly and young they sounded. And that was strange. Actually I was younger than most of them. Why did I feel so much older? Suddenly I didn't want that. I wanted to be gay and excited and maybe as silly as they were. *"I* know," I said mysteriously.

"You *do?* Where?" Hattie asked for all of them.

"St. Louis, of course. Miss Engles . . . Mrs. Evans lived there with her aunt before she came here. Her aunt is dead but she has friends. She went to school there." I waited as they exchanged glances. They didn't believe me. I added, "And after St. Louis they'll probably go on to New York. Mr. Evans was a college professor there, you know."

Donna was still skeptical. "How would *you* know all that? Did they tell you?"

"About the aunt and his being a college professor, yes. About where they are going, no. I reasoned that out. I just imagined where I'd like to go if *I* were married to Mr. Evans."

"Oh, Ann, for pity sake! It's not the same. You're *not* married to Mr. Evans, and you're *not* Miss . . . Mrs. Evans. You don't know a thing more than we do about where they're going. I'll bet . . . ."

"Shhhhh!" Hattie silenced her. Martin was coming over to us.

"Enjoying yourselves, girls?" he asked, then spoke to me. "Ann, Mrs. Evans would like a few words with you before they leave."

The girls looked surprised but no one said anything. I went with Martin down an inner hallway and stopped at a bedroom door. "She's in there, changing for their trip." His eyes smiled. "Was my sermon short enough, Ann?"

"Oh, yes. And very beautiful, Martin. Was your text really from the Song of Solomon?"

"Of course. Did you think I made all that up?" he teased.

"No. I just never realized how beautiful it was before, I guess."

"Neither did I, Ann," he said. "Now you had better see what Mrs. Evans wants. I'll see you later."

She turned as I came into the room. "I'll be just a minute longer, Ann. Please sit down. I thought we might have this little time to ourselves before I leave." She went on putting things into her suitcase. She had changed into a lovely soft-green suit and matching hat. The color seemed reflected in her eyes. Always she looked beautiful. Today she was radiant.

"There I think that's everything. Now we can talk a while."

"The wedding dress? You've forgotten it."

"No, Mrs. Hughes is going to take care of it for me. And this suitcase I've packed. We'll pick up the bags for our trip on the way to the station."

"It's so beautiful," I said. "And so were you Miss . . . Mrs. Evans." We both laughed.

"I have to get used to it too," she said. "But I like the sound of it!"

She sat down on the bed beside me. "I wanted to talk with you about what you intend doing now, Ann. Have you decided to go away to school in the fall?"

"Yes. But I haven't decided where as yet."

She took my hand and held it affectionately for a moment. "I'm sure you know Jim and I have a special fondness for you, Ann. Your future is very important to us. You must let nothing keep you from going on with your education."

"Mama says the same thing but I don't think Papa believes it is very important. He won't forbid it, though. I just haven't decided where to go. I'd like to go to where you went but I'm not sure I want to go that far from home right now. Do you think the Sioux City Academy would be as good as the school in St. Louis?"

"It's smaller, of course. But perhaps that *would* be better— your first time away from home. Besides, it will give all of us a chance to see you more often." She smiled, then added. "But you must not let distance influence your decision unduly, Ann. The important thing is the right school for you. To determine that, you must know what you intend doing with your education. Have you thought about that, my dear?"

Had there been enough time, I think I might have confessed my love for Martin and that I wanted to marry him. "I've thought about it but I'm not quite ready to talk about it. Will you be back before I have to leave for school?"

She hesitated a moment. "Probably not. We haven't told anyone else, except Mr. and Mrs. Hughes, what I'm about to tell you. They will look after Jim's place while we are away. You see, we're going first to St. Louis for a couple of weeks, then on to New York for the rest of the summer. Jim's uncle, his only relative in America, has a place on Long Island Sound. He's spending the summer in England and letting us have his home to ourselves. Isn't that delightful?"

I told her I couldn't imagine anything more wonderful. A

whole summer in a beautiful home near the water! She got up suddenly and went to the small desk and wrote something on one of her calling cards and handed it to me. "If you *had* decided to go to school in St. Louis, I would have made arrangements for you while we are there. Since you haven't, send this to the Dean if you decide that is where you wish to go. He's my friend as well as the Dean."

I thanked her, deeply moved by her thoughtfulness. Who but she would have taken time to consider my welfare while on her wedding trip? I asked, "Will you be teaching at Goldenrod this fall?"

"Oh, yes. I couldn't leave the school without a teacher." She smiled. "Mr. Hughes *says* he's going to need a lot of time to replace me. Whether that's true or not, it *is* nice of him to say it."

"Oh, I'm sure it *is* true!" The words tumbled out.

She hugged me. "Thank you, dear. There's nothing nicer than feeling needed. Jim and I are going to miss you very much. Now we'd better go before Jim begins to think I've left him at the church!" She stepped to the mirror to fix the tilt of her hat and tuck in a stray curl, then picked up her bridal bonquet. "I mustn't forget this. The girls would never forgive me."

We went back to the noisy parlor and found Mr. Evans. I heard him whisper, "You're absolutely ravishing, Mrs. Evans!"

The carriage had been brought around to the parsonage gate. From the looks of it, all the kids in the neighborhood had been very busy. Streamers with tin cans at the end were tied to the back axlerod. Colored streamers decorated the surrey top, and the horses' bridles were bedecked with flowers. Across the back of the surrey was a lettered sign: *Just Married*.

The newlyweds stepped out onto the porch and were greeted by a shower of rice and confetti. A squealing, laughing group of young girls waited for the big moment when the bouquet would be tossed, Vina among them. The couple reached the carriage and got in and Mr. Evans picked up the lines. The horses began to move. Had she forgotten the bridal bouquet afterall? There was a tense moment before she leaned from the surrey and tossed the bouquet into a field of up-stretched arms. Nellie Hughes caught it. She was quickly surrounded by the less fortunate. And catching it must have been lucky for her. She married Tom Simpson in September.

When we got home that evening and Mama unpacked the basket which held her silver service, I saw there was another package. Three pieces of wedding cake for those who had stayed at home.

# CHAPTER XII
## 1896

A relentless August sun burned in a cloudless sky. Heat waves shimmered in motionless air. The dry whirring sound of locust punctuated the Sunday afternoon stillness.

It was cooler here on the front porch shaded by the big cottonwood, but still too hot to keep my thoughts on the book I was reading. I put it aside and lay back in the porch swing, feeling lazy and useless. Living in town was wonderful, but once we had everything moved in and put in place there was so little to do. On the farm there was never enough time. Here there seemed to be too much. Why wasn't there some way to balance time more evenly? And a few other things too. Like heat and cold. Even on the hottest days at the farm there was always a little breeze—except maybe when a cyclone was building up and the air became heavy and still. But this prolonged heat and stillness was different. The sun beat down on dry dusty streets and unshaded buildings. All life seemed to have withered and died today. The streets were empty.

Of course, winters in town would be a lot nicer. No outside work to be done even if a blizzard were raging or the rain coming down in torrents. Nevertheless, I mused, I was going to miss many things on the farm which we often took for granted. The dewy meadows on a spring morning with the smell of fresh new grass and the sound of bird song. And summer evenings watching the sun sink beyond the rosy horizon as I brought the cows in and dusk settled over the prairie. Most of all I would miss autumn's blazing colors and the smell of burning leaves. I supposed they burned leaves in town too, but it wouldn't be the same.

"Living *is* change," Grandma had once said to me. "God intended it to be so."

The past several months had brought many changes in all our lives. Most significant, perhaps, was the great change in Papa. From the moment we started packing to move into the new house he sat in the big Morris chair giving orders to everyone with the same old vigor, although now he was cheerful about it. Mama let him make decisions about some things.

These he pronounced with the solemnity of a man about to possess a new promised land. Even more surprising was that he no longer resisted the idea of using a wheelchair when he got to town.

"It should be here by the time you get settled in," Dr. Matthews told him. "You'll have to continue using some common sense, Sam, but you'll be able to get around the house by yourself. And if you *are* sensible you'll be walking before very long."

Papa accepted the prediction without comment, but we knew he wanted to believe it. He and Uncle Phil were going over the bill of sale for livestock and farm machinery the last morning before we left. "We'll keep the surrey and greys, Phil. That's all the transportation we'll need now. Except that new-fangled go-cart Dr. Matthews insists on putting me into. And, by George, I'm not going to be needing *that* very long!"

"I can believe it. You're doing fine. Before you know it you'll be prancing around again on your own two legs."

Our furniture was loaded, and Uncle Phil's unloaded and put in place. The house looked strange and empty without Mama's nice things, but Uncle Phil said it would be comfortable. "Everything Fred and I need, and more, even if it's not as pretty as it was."

"It will be—when Fred brings home a bride," Mama laughed.

"Which won't be for a long time," Fred vowed. "Pa and I have enough to do taking care of this big farm without having a woman underfoot."

"You'll sing another tune when you meet the right girl," Grandma said.

Vina and Lucy and I went through the house to make sure we hadn't forgotten anything. When we came downstairs Uncle Ethan and Aunt Hilda and their children were there, with Mrs. Wiley.

"Couldn't let you folks git away without sayin' goodbye," Mrs. Wiley said. "Lan' sakes, Mrs. Bullard, we're sure gonna miss all of you like ev'rything! But I reckon you'll like livin' in town. 'Specially in that fancy Stebbins house."

Mama smiled. "I don't know how fancy it is, Mrs. Wiley, but it certainly is roomy. It's so nice of you to come over to see us off."

"That's part the reason I come. Want t' talk to Mr. Phillips, too." She turned to him. "I've been thinkin' you an' the boy'll likely be needin' someone t' keep the place fit to live in. Men don't know beans 'bout keepin' house. Except th' Reverend, that is. *He's* neat as a pin. Hardly no work a-tall takin' care o' *his* house. Mondays're my wash day, and I do the cleanin' on Friday so's things'll be nice for Sunday, and I do my bakin' on Saturday. So if yo' want, I kin come Tuesday or Thursday an' clean up for ye. 'Corse you'd have to fetch me and get me back in time t' make supper for th' Reverend. I won't charge much." The long speech had left her breathless.

Uncle Phil pulled on his pipe, "How does Rev. Pritchard feel about this?"

"Oh, it'll be all right with him. T' be right honest 'bout it, t'was his *idee*."

"What do you think, Fred?"

"Pa, I'd drive half across the state to get Mrs. Wiley if I never have to wash another dish or make another bed!"

Papa laughed. "Weren't you the young man who just said he didn't want a woman underfoot?"

Fred's face got red. "You know what I mean. Mrs. Wiley's different."

"All right, Mrs. Wiley. Let's make it Thursday. That way we'll have some clean dishes for Sunday. And be sure to thank Rev. Pritchard for us."

In final farewell to the farm, all of us gathered around the kitchen table for coffee and some of the cakes Aunt Hilda had brought. She also presented Uncle Phil and Fred with two loaves of freshly-baked bread, assuring them that these assured prosperity and long life to the new occupants. Altogether it was a merry occasion. Aunt Hilda kept it lively, reminding us of funny things that had happened since we moved onto the farm. Like the time Mae and Hans found "a pretty black kitty with a white stripe", and tried to bring it home.

"Phew! I still smell the stink! Hans I wash and wash and he still smell. His clothes I burn."

Mama had done the same with Mae and her clothes. "She still runs and hides if she sees a black cat."

"An' the time I kidnap you and *kinder* from soddy and Sam fall *mit* face in snow! Like snowman you look, Sam. Big, *very* mad snowman!"

Papa laughed about it now, but he hadn't laughed then; nor had we.

"Ja!" Aunt Hilda sighed. "Goot times ve haf'. Now you move to fine house in town." She shrugged, and smiled. "But you still goot friends. You bring us nice neighbors, too. Already my Kathy crazy in love mit you, Fred."

"Well, you tell Kathy I'm crazy in love with her too. I'm just waiting for her to grow up so I can propose."

"*You* t'ink so. Hilda t'ink you have no chance to wait. Too many pretty girls be settin' cap for you *and* your papa."

"You hear that, Phil?" Uncle Ethan put in. "If Hilda has her way she'll have you both married before snow flies."

"Vy not? Man need voman in his house."

"You're right there," Papa said.

"Oh, ja? You talk different now, Sam Bullard! Vat goot girls to farmers, huh?" she reminded him, and laughed.

Papa's face got red, but he laughed too. "Well, one thing's sure, Hilda. In town I won't have to listen to your tongue lashings. And if I had my strength I'd turn you over my knee right here, and show you who's boss!"

The very idea of Papa spanking Aunt Hilda made everyone laugh. She was almost as big as he was.

Mama's beautiful furniture, which now she admitted had been a little out of place in a farmhouse, was just right for the new house. To it she had added Brussels rugs for the dining-room and downstairs bedroom, and carpeting for the hall and stairway. No straw matting went under these. Long strips of building paper from the hardware store, several layers thick, provided soft cushioning. The part of the floors that showed around the rugs was polished until it shone like a mirror. For the dining-room and living-room there were new lace curtains, and brocaded draperies for the parlor.

As planned, one downstairs room became a temporary bedroom for Papa until he was able to manage the stairs. Then Mama would have both a parlor and a library. The front bedroom upstairs was now Grandma's room. Lucy and Mae shared a room, but Vina and I had our own rooms. I'd chosen the one over the back porch because it was smaller and cozier, and it had casement windows which swung outward, giving a wonderful view of the prairies beyond the town. The other upstairs bedroom would become Mama's and Papa's room when he was able to use the stairs. All the beds now had cotton-filled mattresses; no more straw ticking!

Vina and I, with Lucy tagging along, had had a wonderful time exploring the new place. There were many things we hadn't noticed that first day in our excitement. Back of the house was a garden patch with brown tendrils of last year's beans and tomato vines showing through fresh new greens. Beyond it was the "carriage house", and farther back where the ground sloped slightly downward, was the barn. The carriage house was new and exciting. It had a real stairway, not a ladder, which led to a neatly constructed hayloft. It was empty of hay now, and the floor was covered with dust. Its windows, also dust-streaked, looked onto the garden and the backyard.

"Won't this be a wonderful playhouse?" Lucy exclaimed, making footprints in the dust. "When it's cleaned up, of course."

"It's for hay and grain, silly," Vina said.

However, to our surprise, Papa agreed that Lucy and Mae could use the front half of the loft for a playhouse. The back would be enough room for all the hay and grain the greys needed. "But be careful of that stairwell, kids." It was open to permit bales of hay and bags of grain to be hoisted up for storing.

As soon as the house was in order Mama began spending more time at the hardware store. Vina and I planted the garden with radishes, lettuce, beans and onions, and added some tomato vines to those already there. We planted flowers along the front fence and next to the house on each side of the porch. Zinnias, marigolds and nasturtiums in the front yard, with beds of pansies and sweet-peas under the dining-room windows. Tall hollyhocks grew along the back fence.

Taking care of the yards and garden soon fell to me. Vina was always finding an excuse to stop in at the hardware store and spend most of the afternoon there until Mama put a stop to it. But that didn't stop Donald. Soon he was asking permission to take her to Jason's Ice Cream Parlor on Sunday afternoons. Papa tried to refuse, but not very firmly. Mama gave her consent. Sometimes in the evenings when Dr. Matthews stopped in to check Papa's progress, Donald was with him. I hoped Gus hadn't been too fond of Vina. *She* certainly wasn't losing any sleep over him!

We had been living in town almost three weeks before Martin stopped by to see us. Papa now got around easily in his wheel chair. He answered the door. And greeted Martin as though there had never been a breach between them, plying him with questions about things in the community and how Phil and Fred were doing. Later, Mama served tea in the sitting-room, and Martin had a chance to express enthusiasm for the grandeur of our new home.

"But we all miss you. Couldn't you all come out on Friday for Literary meeting? There's going to be an especially fine program, and you haven't been out since you moved to town. We're beginning to feel slighted." He glanced quickly at me and smiled.

"You don't mean that!" Mama chided. "We miss those good times very much, but it is still too soon for Sam to make such a long drive. He's doing fine, as you can see. We have to be patient a while longer."

Papa admitted Mama was right about that. "But you can bet if I wasn't stuck in this confounded chair, we'd be there!"

"Can I persuade you, Ann? I'll be delighted to drive in for you Friday evening."

"Can't you see she doesn't need any persuading, Martin?" Papa laughed.

I was embarrassed by this bluntness, but forgave him. It was such a miracle to have him on speaking terms with Martin, and *urging* me to go out with him!

Thereafter, Martin called for me almost every Friday night (unless some rare emergency prevented it). At Literary meeting he maintained a decorum befitting his position as minister, paying equal attention to everyone. But most of them no longer whispered about me; they took it for granted that I was his "girl", and behaved accordingly. I knew some of them wanted to ask questions but not even Donna, who was usually very outspoken, seemed to have the courage to do it.

For Martin and me the long ride home was time that belonged only to us. It did not matter that we were not permitted to join in the dancing after the program was over. His arm was around me on the ride home. The horse followed the familiar road. Here we could talk and laugh without inquisitive glances. Often we rode in silence, happy just being together.

The summer days had drifted by in so much pure contentment that sometimes it seemed impossible to contain all of it. And I thought about how much of it we owed to Grandpa's thoughtfulness and Mama's courage and wisdom in using the inheritance. And of how much more we owed to faith and God's guidance. I was also old enough now to understand Papa a great deal better, and why there were so many times when he seemed mean and cruel. He had had the daring to "pioneer", although often he had seemed inconsiderate of Mama and us, and had forced his ways upon us. But Papa had always worked hard; he knew no other way. Mama had had Grandma and Grandpa to provide better things while she was growing up. Now, with more mature perspective, I considered whether Papa had not also contributed greatly to this time of security and contentment *because* of his irresistible urge to "pioneer". Were the changes he had forced us to make perhaps steps toward this better time in our lives?

Life was, indeed, now made up of many changes! Many of these, of course, Mama directed into smooth-flowing patterns of growth and purpose. Music lessons with the best teacher in town; church and Sunday school where we made new friends and learned town ways. Gradually we were becoming a significant part of Stebbinsville life. Mama could entertain her friends graciously as she had been taught, and now was teaching us. We had a fine home in which to receive our friends and gentlemen callers—a dream of hers for us, fulfilled. I wondered if Elsie would have been any happier than she was now had she waited for this time; to wear the fine clothes she had dreamed about, to be courted properly and given a fine wedding; and to know that Papa had meant only the best for us however rough his way of showing it. Seeing Elsie and Jed and Davy together, I knew she could not be happier. How, I thought, could one determine the value of things while growing up? Maybe love *was* all that mattered.

It was almost the middle of July before Papa was able to walk again. He still had to use crutches to steady himself, but Dr. Matthews assured him he wouldn't have to use them very long. "Just long enough to get your leg muscles strengthened."

It was during this leg-strengthening period that Mama tactfully began to prepare Papa in other ways for the new life ahead of him. "Papa's been out of things so long he's lost his own sense of importance," she told me. I hadn't particularly noticed *that!* "While he was more or less helpless he was willing to accept the situation. Now that he's back on his feet he's likely to get pretty cranky unless he has something to keep him busy."

She didn't mention what she had in mind to accomplish this, but a week or so later she brought it up while she and Papa were talking after supper. He was reading the weekly paper, commenting now and then on the news, while Mama occupied herself with her sewing basket. It had been a very hot day. The rest of us had escaped to the cooler front porch, but even here it was too hot to talk. We listened lazily to their conversation, not really hearing anything until Papa raised his voice.

"By gad! That McKinley's sure a real fighter. And a good thing too. We've no business getting mixed up in that Cuba fracas."

Mama agreed. "We do seem to have enough problems of our own right here at home." And a moment later added, "In fact, Sam, I've been meaning to talk to you about one of *ours.*"

He chuckled. "I didn't know we had any problems these days."

"Not a very big one, I suppose. It's about Donald. You remember it was temporary when we hired him; just until Dr. Matthews' practice was large enough to need his help. It seems it *is* big enough now. Donald would like to leave the hardware store as soon as we can get someone to replace him."

"I don't see that's any problem. I'm perfectly capable of running the store myself now. Or don't you agree?"

"I don't question your ability, Sam. But are you sure you can be on your feet that much?"

"Of course I'm sure. It'll be good to be busy again. I wasn't cut out for this lazy life I've been forced to endure."

"Well, if you're sure I'll speak to Donald tomorrow."

"Are *you* sure, Mrs Bullard, you can trust me not to give away all the profits?" Papa teased.

"Oh, Sam! You know that wasn't the reason I hired Donald. You were needed on the farm. Now you're needed here. I just want to be sure you're well enough, that's all."

"Yes, Molly. I'm well enough. And let me tell you something else. This town life's pretty danged nice at that!"

And it was. For all of us. Papa was happier than he'd been in a long time, spending his days at the store, and feeling important enough to satisfy himself *and* Mama. He rarely lost his temper the way he used to do, and accepted the fact that we were growing up and were old enough to have gentlemen callers.

Lying here in the porch swing on this hot August day, trying to keep cool, I remembered that cold day in February, more than seven years ago, when we had arrived in Stebbinsville and Papa, the pioneer, was not there to meet us. And the awful soddy with buried bones, and the years of hard work under hot sun and through freezing weather. With Mama's faith, and our own, we had survived those years and she had kept alive our hope for better times until she and Papa could make them reality.

Now, very soon, I would be leaving for the Academy in Sioux City. It had required many hours of argument with myself to make that decision, and the biggest point in its favor was its nearness to home—and Martin. For weeks, now, Mama and Grandma had been busy making my new clothes. Some days I was excited about this new life that lay ahead of me; others, I dreaded the strangeness of it . . . . .

Grandma came out onto the porch, scattering my thoughts. She had a pitcher of lemonade and a glass. "I just made it. Thought you'd like some."

"I sure would. Thanks." I sat up and sipped from the tall glass. "Ummmm! It tastes as cool as it looks. Is August this hot in Roanoke?"

"August is hot anywhere, I guess—except maybe at the North Pole."

"On the farm Papa called August 'the dog-days'."

"Do you know why they're called that?"

"Not really, I guess. Unless it's because they make you feel as lazy as an old dog. The way I feel today."

"That may have something to do with it. Dogs *are* more affected by heat than humans. Did you ever see a mad-dog, Ann?"

"No, and I hope I never do. I've heard about them."

"It's the intense heat that makes him mad. He froths at the mouth and even the gentlest dog is dangerous then. If he bites you, you could get rabies and that's almost certain death."

"How awful! Have you ever seen one, Grandma?"

"Many times. It's not a pleasant sight. Folks stayed indoors until someone shot the poor animal and dragged it away and buried it."

I shuddered. "I'm glad now Papa never would let us have a dog on the farm."

"Did he ever tell you why?"

"Papa didn't tell us *why* about anything. He just said no and that ended it."

Grandma sat down beside me in the swing. "Maybe it's time you knew why. I used to wonder about your father not liking dogs. Farm folk usually do. One day I asked him. He said it wasn't dogs he disliked, only what could happen to them. And he told me what had happened to his."

He was twelve, Grandma said, when he got his first dog and his first gun for Christmas. It was hard to tell which he loved the most. They hunted together, chased squirrels and 'possums, and the dog slept on the foot of his bed. Papa had lived in Georgia then, she said. "And there's no hotter place in the world I know of than Georgia in August."

That first August after Papa got the dog was a real scorcher. One day the dog disappeared. Papa searched everywhere for it. Then about the middle of the afternoon his mother started for the well and the dog came at her from behind the barn, frothing at the mouth and snarling.

"Your father knew about mad-dogs, and he knew how much danger his mother was in. Much as he loved that dog, he grabbed his gun and shot it. He never trusted another dog, and I guess he never stopped grieving over what he had had to do."

164

"Oh, poor Papa! Why didn't he tell us about this? We always thought he was just mean not wanting us to have a dog."

Grandma got up. "Well, that's enough gloom for today. Finish your lemonade then come upstairs and try on your new dress. I want to finish it tomorrow."

"Do you have to go back to Roanoke, Grandma?"

"Yes, dear. A body shouldn't wear out her welcome, visiting too long."

"You could never do that. We love you."

She leaned and kissed my cheek, then took the pitcher and went inside.

The dress she wanted me to try on was the last of my new school clothes. I'd never before had so many lovely things. All the time they were being made and fitted I was excited about going away to school and living in a big place like Sioux City. But when the dresses were finished and awaited packing in my new suitcases, going away suddenly became almost frightening. Would Martin forget me, the way Vina quickly forgot Gus when Donald began paying attention to her? There were several girls in the farm community who would welcome a chance to win Martin. I felt sure I was the girl he loved, but he hadn't said so. Not in so many words.

Uusually these argument with myself went unresolved as something else momentarily claimed my attention. Today it was trying on the last of the new dresses.

As the time drew near for Grandma to leave all of us pleaded with her to stay, at least until after Christmas.

"I'd like to. You know that. But there are things at home that need doing. Winter's not far off even if it doesn't seem much like it now." However, she finally agreed to stay until I left for school. And a few days later when I heard her talking with Mama, I knew that Mama had found another solution.

"No, it wouldn't be right, Molly," Grandma was saying. "You and Sam have waited a long time for a nice home like this. Besides, I'm kinda set in my ways. A body gets that way at my age."

"The children are growing up, Mother. Before we know it they'll have homes and families of their own. This is a big house, too big for Sam and me. There'd be plenty of room for you 'to be set in your ways' without being lonely."

"I'm grateful to you, daughter, but I guess I'm too used to my own house to want it any other way. I *would* like to be nearer you and Sam and the children. I do get kinda lonely now your father's gone."

Both were silent for a while. Then Mama asked, "Why not sell your house in Roanoke and buy one here? I'm sure Mr. Close can find one for you. If not, he'll just build one for you; he's *that* accommodating!"

"I wouldn't be the least surprised!"

"Will you think about it—I mean about selling your house?"

"Yes. It's a very tempting idea."

"Then do it, Mother. There isn't a reason in the world why you should stay in Roanoke now, except for memories, and you can bring them with you."

"All right. Let's get Ann off to school, then we'll see about it." She lowered her voice. "Do you think Rev. Pritchard is serious about Ann? He's been seeing her a lot lately."

"Perhaps," Mama said. "Ann's a very attractive young woman and more serious-minded than most girls her age. But she is still too young to be serious about anyone. Besides, she has schooling to think about now."

Grandma didn't give up. "May I remind you, daughter, that *you* married Sam when you were her age."

"Things were different then. Marriage was the only career for a properly brought up young lady. Now a girl has a choice. Not that I regret the choice I made, Mother. Sam has not always been easy to live with but I haven't met a man yet I'd trade him for!"

"You've been good for him, Molly. Tempered him, so to speak. Your father used to say Sam expected the Lord to take orders from him once he'd made up his mind to something. And *I* told him Sam was just plain stubborn."

"Would you want a man who wasn't? Most of the time Sam's bluster was more hot air than steam."

Listening, I thought of the "burr" which had pestered Papa for such a long time, and how patiently Mama had waited for him to let it be removed. And I understood why she had been patient all those years, moving from place to place, working too hard, making the best of what we had. She *loved* Papa the way I loved Martin.

# CHAPTER XIII
## 1896

There were times, however, when I was tortured by doubts concerning Martin's real feelings toward me. Did he also consider me too young to be in love? Perhaps his attentions were merely those of a good friend, as Mr. Evans' had been. This possibility turned my stomach into a bottomless well! I knew the difference between love and friendship now. What I felt for Martin was very different from the way I had felt toward Mr. Evans. *This* was love. Certainly I was old enough to know my own heart!

What I did not know was whether Martin felt the same way. Was he really in love with me, the kind of "in love" that would last forever? Only he could answer that, and now the time for answering was growing short. In less than two weeks I'd be leaving for Sioux City.

All through the week I wrestled with indecision. One minute I would decide to give up the Academy altogether and remain in Stebbinsville. The next I knew that education was more important than ever *if* Martin loved me and wanted to marry me. A minister's wife needed more education than the wife of a farmer or merchant. And Martin would not always be preaching in a country church.

Occasionally, when the controversy with myself became too confusing I was tempted to talk to Mama about it, but pride restrained me. She thought I was too young even to be considering marriage. But more than that, I somehow felt this was a decision that I alone must make. It was a part of being old enough, and wise enough, to know whether you were in love enough to want to consider marriage. So I did not ask advice from anyone.

Friday came at last—the last time I would see Martin before leaving for Sioux City. It had been a week of uncertainty, and now this final day seemed endless. But I had made up my mind to find out how Martin felt toward me, even if I had to *ask* him!

Martin would come for me at seven. I put on one of my

prettiest new dresses and watched from the upstairs hall window for his surrey.Suddenly it was there, and he was tieing the mare at the hitching post, and striding up our front walk. He seemed taller tonight, and very handsome in a dark suit and straw hat. I hurried back to my room for a final look at myself. Everything must be perfect tonight. The dress was of emerald-green silk with a fitted bodice and full skirt which almost touched the floor. My hair was done in a high pompadour, and the hat had been made by Miss Millie especially for the dress. Maybe, I thought, these were a little too fancy to wear to a country Literary meeting, but if I didn't wear them tonight Martin would never see me in them—not for a long time anyway.

I could hear him talking with Mama and Papa in the sitting-room, but waited a little while longer for the sake of propriety. "A young lady who wishes to impress her young gentleman does *not* permit herself to appear impatient." How many times Grandma had said that to us girls!

At last I walked slowly down the stairs. Martin came to the foot of the stairway to greet me. "Good evening, Miss Bullard," he said with mock formality, bowing. "You're very lovely tonight."

For a moment I wasn't sure whether he was teasing or serious, then I caught the twinkle in his eyes. "Thank you, kind sir!" I countered. We both laughed.

Mama said, "I thought Martin was taking you to Literary Society tonight, Ann?"

"He is. Why?"

"Isn't that a rather formal dress for an informal occasion?"

Martin answered for me. "Perhaps it is, Mrs. Bullard. But with Ann's permission, I should like the pleasure of her company at dinner at the Stebbins House." He turned to me. "May I, Ann?"

Papa broke up the charade with, "If *you* don't, Martin, I will. You sure do look mighty pretty in that new dress, Ann." It was the nicest thing he could have said to give me confidence.

The Stebbins House had changed considerably since the day we had rested up in one of the rooms after our long train trip. Or perhaps my own sense of awareness had changed. We had seen little of the hotel that day, but I remembered Elsie's fanciful descriptions of dance-hall girls and drummers, and gun-carrying cowhands. None of them was in evidence tonight. The dining-room was softly lighted, and there were white tablecloths and flowers on each table, and violin and piano music which was simply heavenly. Waiters in uniforms served the fashionably dressed diners.

We were escorted to a table near a window. Only now I knew that Martin had planned this evening for at least a week; he'd had no intention of taking me to Literary Society tonight. The waiter took our order and left.

"It's lovely, Martin. Simply lovely!"

"Yes, isn't it? I wanted you to like it, too."

"How could I not like it? And you *didn't* bring me here just because I was wearing this fancy dress."

"It's a beautiful dress, and most becoming. And this is a very special occasion. Do you realize this is perhaps the last time I shall see you before you leave?"

"Yes. I've thought about that a lot."

The musicians were playing a waltz now, and the dance floor was quickly filled. I ached to dance with Martin, and I was pretty sure he felt the same way. But I admired him even more for holding to the principle he had set for himself here. In another place, or another town, where people saw these things differently, Martin could follow the dictates of his own conscience. But here restraint for the sake of others was right.

It was after ten when we left the hotel. A three-quarter moon washed the sky with silver. The deep summer night seemed enchanted. A light breeze had sprung up, stirring the branches of the elms which made a canopy above us. We walked home along a quiet street where moonlight lay in dappled patterns. Yellow leaves drifted down. We did not talk. Words would surely have broken the magic spell.

The house was dark when we reached our front gate. In the dim cavern of the porch, the swing cast a silver shadow in the moonlight.

"May I come up for a while?"

For answer I pushed open the gate. We tiptoed up the walk and onto the porch, and sat down cautiously in the swing lest its creak awaken Papa. He slept lightly, not yet accustomed to town noises. I noticed that tonight the bedroom window opening onto the porch was closed. I pointed to it.

"It's all right. We don't have to whisper." Grandma had probably closed that window. *She* didn't think I was too young to be in love!

We sat there for a long while, his arm around me, saying nothing. When he spoke I knew he had been searching for the right words, and maybe the courage to say them. "I've wanted to tell you many times what is in my heart, Ann. I have loved you even before you were old enough to know what those words meant. Now I must say them because you'll be going away, and I couldn't bear to have you go without knowing how I feel about you." He took my hand, caressing it. "I'm asking you to marry me, darling."

I sat very still, not daring to believe what I had heard. All doubts were suddenly washed away. He loved me! He wanted to marry me!

He must have misinterpreted my silence. He said quietly," I know you are too young to be sure now, dearest. And I know the Academy is important and right for you. I won't be as selfish as I'd like to be, and ask you to give that up; but I've been tempted to a dozen times. If you love me, Ann, I can wait."

"Oh, Martin, I do, I do! I'll never, never love anyone else!"

He kissed me and held me close for a long time. The muted sound of the clock striking eleven reminded us where we were.

"I must let you go in now, darling. I shall come tomorrow to ask your parents' blessings on our engagement."

A tremor of fear went through me. Would they give their blessings? Quickly I put the fear from me. Nothing must mar the wonder of this night.

He leaned and kissed me good-night. "Until tomorrow, darling," he whispered.

I watched until he waved and drove away. Then let myself into the silent house. I was much too filled with happiness for sleep. Until long after midnight I sat at the window of my room looking out across the prairie, dimly shadowed in the moonlight. The doubts of the past week were gone; there remained only the question of Mama's and Papa's blessings. Surely, I thought, they would understand that we really loved each other and would want us to be happy. It wasn't as if

Martin were asking me to give up school and marry him to-morrow. He asked only the right to wait for me until I finished school.

Suddenly the moon-shadowed prairies were those four years stretching ahead of me, endlessly. Four years of waiting and learning before I could become Martin's wife. How could I ever endure them? How could I keep my mind on learning when it would be filled with thoughts of him? And then I remembered that there would be summers and holidays together. But these would be all too brief, and four years still seemed like a century!

At last I went to bed and lay there remembering every beautiful moment of the evening. And I knew, as surely as I could know anything, that our love for each other was deep and good and that marriage, in its own time, would have God's blessing too.

And I thought of something I had read in one of Mr. Evans' philosophy books: "True happiness between two people comes from a blending of mind and spirit, loving and sharing, growing in wisdom together."

This was the life I wanted to share with Martin. Those four years at the Academy would prepare me for it. Surely patience was a small price to pay for a lifetime of happiness!

The end

The story of **Ann of the Prairie** continues in Volume 3 (*These Years of Promise*) and Volume 4 (*While Yet We Live*) of the series. Also don't miss our **Stories of Yesteryear** series of turn-of-the-century stories by the best-selling author Ralph Connor. Both series are available through your local Christian bookstore.

## A WORD FROM
## THE PUBLISHER

We at Sunrise Books have a special commitment to you, the reader, in offering you a quality, wholesome book.

If this book has been such for you, we would encourage you to try another Sunrise Book. Your local bookstore is the first place to check for all your book needs. If they are unable to help you, or if there's not a bookstore convenient for you, we would be proud to serve you.

Sunrise Books
1707 E Street
Eureka, CA 95501